CAPTURED

HEARTS

WAYNE P. WATSON

&

LEE TETER

BLACK ROSE
writing™

The final approval for this literary material is granted by the author.

First printing

This is a work of fiction. Names, characters, businesses, places, events and incidents are either the products of the author's imagination or used in a fictitious manner. Any resemblance to actual persons, living or dead, or actual events is purely coincidental.

ISBN: 978-1-61296-685-4
PUBLISHED BY BLACK ROSE WRITING
www.blackrosewriting.com

Printed in the United States of America
Suggested retail price $15.95

Captured Hearts is printed in Adobe Caslon Pro

To those re-enactors not satisfied to let history pass without notice, and in memory of John and Jane Frazer, who's story this is.

CAPTURED

HEARTS

CAPTURED HEARTS

BY WAYNE P. WATSON
AND LEE TETER

Wayne P. Watson

Lee Teter

PROLOGUE

July 20, 2016
Bedford County, Pennsylvania

The young boys abandoned the baseball to the black opening in the farmhouse window and ran away. Shards littered the floor of the attic and sparkled across the dusty shapes and forms of neglected and forgotten things. A trunk from 1918 was the resting place for a dusty case that held a pair of roller skates. The skates had delighted a young girl in 1958. Beside it sat a record player and a stack of albums that gave a married woman relief from the surrounding country quiet in 1966. The layers of dust, gobs of bees nests, shed snake skins, and ten thousand grain-like mouse droppings had deterred human activity for at least a hundred years. Ten years of dust covered the only visible footprints as they led to and from a 35 mm Pentax camera that had been boxed in 1999 and shoved deep into the shadows.

The grass stained baseball lay beside the camera box. Its white leather reflected light from the broken window so brilliantly in the dimness of the room that it seemed to glow. That reflected light bounced upward against the rafters and caught on dust the hovered in the air. The light also caught on delicately carved scroll work and tiny leaves and flowers that had been carved into a slender maple gun stock. The antique gun had been jammed into the rafters 140 years ago when the house was newly built by inherited money. The gun, already ancient when the house was built, had been inherited too. It was placed high in the attic to keep it from the children, and there it rested until the baseball came rolling to a stop beneath it.

No one remembered how the trunk had carried all the worldly possessions of a German girl when she moved to America at the age of 12. No one thought about the skates that brought a thousand smiles to a girl in 1958. No one made notes on the backs of photos taken by the camera. And the stories about the rifle had died with those who knew them.

But everything has a story. The rifle had one too. Only stories have beginnings and the story of the rifle started two centuries ago and half a continent away...

CHAPTER ONE

The year 1755

First the girl died...

In a bark-covered shelter at the southern edge of the great lakes an Indian woman lay trying to survive. The woman had been in labor for long hours. Her strength was failing rapidly. Perhaps the pregnancy would have gone easier if small pox had not recently weakened her. Half-healed sores still covered her body. The disease had carried her husband away, and she had moved back to her mother's lodge even before she could complete the period of mourning for him: She had to think of the welfare of her unborn child. This young woman, still in her teens, had much sadness, fear, and concern. She had much love for the child in her belly, but she was so tired.

The 50 years that just passed had brought a staggering amount of change to the Indian people of North America. The trade so coveted by the tribes had created new priorities for the people, and old knowledge and old values disappeared in a few generations. For this young woman, it brought tragedy in the form of small pox. In exchange for two otter skins, her husband got an old blanket and the sickness. He died, leaving her alone and frightened.

The pain was becoming unbearable. Herbs that should ease the pain failed. Her family sent a messenger to find the conjurer. The tattooed and grizzled old man bragged about the life-saving miracles he could make. Payment must be made, so the messenger presented him with that most popular trade item, cloth. After a few questions, the tattooed old man nodded and went to get his tools. Perhaps there was still time for his secrets to save the girl.

Carrying his powers in various pouches of animal skins he came to the girl. He used the powers in his songs, used the words and rhythms carried in his head or written in signs on a birch bark scroll, but nothing worked. When the girl was beyond the point of recognizing the conjurer he evicted her female attendants. As they waited outside the shelter, they saw smoke and heard songs covered by the sounds of a rattle. Then the singing stopped. Only the moans of the girl were heard. Hours passed.

Deep in the night the conjurer appeared outside and said there was no hope. He had asked for help from the spirits but was refused. The girl would die. The old man had spoken.

The mother went to her daughter and cried. An hour later Catches-the-Wind was gone.

Her death was announced throughout the village by women specially appointed to do so. Within minutes after she died, these women walked through the village shouting, "She is no more! She is no more!"

The following day the entire village went into mourning. Cries and lamentations could be heard as the women spread the news. The mourners and spectators came and went all night, some gave support to the grief stricken mother, while others gained needed sympathy. By the next morning, Catches-the-Wind lay on a huge piece of bark dressed in the finest new clothing available; after all, she was a sister of a war chief of high standing within the tribe. She was painted in the most superb manner — Her garments were set off with rows of silver broaches, one row joining the other. She had silver bands on each arm. Her long black hair had been wrapped in red flannel, and a series of silver hair plates in graduated sizes covered the hair wrap, with the red of the flannel showing through the piercings of each hair plate. Many strings of wampum hung around her neck, each string a different length, forming a kind of breastplate over her printed trade cloth gown. Her scarlet leggings were decorated with different colored beads, the outer edges sewn with yellow trade silk and many tin cones were sown close together with tufts of red dyed deer hair bursting from each cone. Her moccasins were ornamented with colored porcupine quills, sewn in careful designs, and many small silver bells were sewn around the flaps of her garters. She was beautiful. They hadn't given her over to death just because she died.

A number of articles were brought out of the lodge and placed in the bark coffin; a small brass pot containing a looking glass, a sewing kit, a knife, a spoon and a cup. A piece of dressed deer skin was placed next to the pot for new shoes to be made when she needed them. Other small things Catches-the-Wind had been fond of were placed in the coffin and the lid was tied on. Each end had been stopped up, but a small hole had been cut into one end so her spirit could pass into and out of the coffin during her search for a place of eternal residence. A small bag of vermilion paint was thrust into the coffin through the hole that had been cut.

Finally, the bearers lifted Catches-the-Wind for the journey to her grave. Several women carried pots and kettles of food. Other women acting as chief mourners made wailing sounds, even if there were no tears, and cut the air with their shrill cries. War chiefs and counselors followed the family and the coffin. Several rest stops had to be made. Now and then there were quiet sobs or a grief stricken groan that served to keep the girl's mother feeling sorrow fresh with each step.

At the grave site men stepped forward and the moaning sounds from the women mourners reached a fever pitch. Dirt was thrown up so it would fall down on their heads. Women pulled at their hair and wailed in loud voices, calling for Catches-the-Wind to rise and not abandon them. At last the coffin was tied so tight that only a spirit could move in and out of it. Then it was lowered into the ground while the sounds of wailing fell low, but the women still pulled at their clothing, and pulled grass and dirt and threw it over themselves in grief. A painted post, on which were drawn figures symbolic of the girl's station in life, was brought forward and placed at the head of the coffin in such a position that certain of the stick figures were exposed to the rising sun. While the post was held in place, dirt filled the grave and secured the post in an upright position. Logs enclosed the grave site breast high to protect it from wild animals.

Food carried to the grave site was passed out and eaten; no one from the oldest to the youngest was excepted. After everyone had eaten, gifts were passed out, the women who had been the mourners received the most prominent gifts, and indeed they had earned them.

As it grew dark, a kettle of food was placed within the barrier of logs. This was done every evening for three weeks and each evening the sobs and wailings of the mourners could be heard, though not so loud as each preceding evening. At the end of this period of time, it was assumed that the departed had found her way to the great spirit and was in company with the loved ones who had passed on before her.

The girl's mother was an old woman about forty years old. She wanted grandchildren but Catches-the-Wind was gone and her surviving daughter was barren. The white man's disease had caused this sorrow too. She took her sorrow to her son, Kitcheogeemaw. This young man was required to enforce justice in the family, and it was his duty to honor the wishes of his mother. She told him, "Go to the white men and bring a woman to take the place of Catches-the-Wind; it is only right that they should lose a daughter to restore my own."

Kitcheogeemaw agreed and left to purify himself. He was a successful leader and many warriors were willing to join him. Together they purified themselves in the sweat lodge and performed songs and rituals given to each individual. They performed the dances and would not touch women or certain foods. They painted in special ways. On the fourth day they were ready.

An old Indian stood at a distance and watched as the war party prepared and left. The wise old Indian standing was named Jacob by the whites. He was afraid of the sadness the war parties would bring upon his people. He could not have known this war party would bring results that would warm his old heart...if only for a little while.

The old man recognized the losing fight his people were involved in. Jacob had been educated by the whites, but he was of his people and they were part of him. Sure, his tribe fought to protect their lands but their reasons for fighting went deeper than that. If men were men at all it was required of them by their culture: They needed to prove they were brave because cowardice could mean destruction to their tribe. Even deeper: Their beliefs guided them to please certain spirits and redeem the souls of their dead in a ritual that white men would consider revenge. Others, like Kitcheogeemaw's party, went to war to replace a dead member of a family; or simply to give an old woman a daughter to love again.

The people of the village stood to watch the men leave. The warriors had prepared themselves for death more than for killing. They had painted and prayed. They yelled and hallooed and fired off their guns. It was a sight to behold. The women were supportive because they were supposed to be, but a closer look would reveal the worry in their faces.

Outside the village the men stopped and peeled a big section of bark from a tree. On the slick pale wood where the bark had been removed they painted their memorial. The tree would tell who led the group, how many were in it, and the clan sign of each warrior. At this place they removed much of their fine clothing and some of their decorated ceremonial gear, then the green foliage of the forest swallowed them up, leaving only a peeled tree and strange markings to remember them if they never returned again.

CHAPTER 2

The Phares' homestead near Fort Cumberland

Rachel was playing with puppies. Wearing a mid-calf length skirt that would be appalling east of the mountains, her hair was loose and her bare feet were dirty. She was still a barely tame girl whose surroundings demanded that she become a woman. Mamma dog watched Rachel as she giggled and played with the pups. There were horses in the distance and a tangle of pack saddles hung in a crude shelter. Chickens searched for seeds and bugs along the log walls of the cabin and a hog grunted from beyond the fence. A mile or so beyond that fence flowed a river that would someday mark the southern boundary of western Maryland.

Nineteen-year-old Rachel Phares had seen much toil and heartache on the frontier, and yet there was a softness about her in spite of the hard life she led. Her graceful movements and childlike innocence merged to present a great contrast with the typical hardening of frontier life. She had seen terror but she was stronger, more elegant, than terror. There was only one man who knew the fears she hid from the rest of the world: She loved her husband, John, with all her being.

A rifle shot broke the quiet and Rachel jumped. This rifle shot, as did all gun shots, instantly sent her mind spinning through the years to another day near Winchester, Virginia when she was a little girl.

· · ·

That day had been warm, much like this day, but began to cool toward evening. Rachel could see her older brother watching the cows as they ambled across the field with their bells clanking and udders almost painfully full of milk. She knew his eyes were searching the growing shadows in the tree line, always aware of danger that could be nearby. Seeing nothing, he turned toward the log cabins that had been surrounded by palisades as a defense. Four families from the nearby valley lived there. Rachel's brother gripped a smoothbore flintlock in his calloused hands as he walked back toward their cabin and a half-finished barn.

Rachel was playing with her friends that day, and their laughter blended with the sounds of the women bickering, scolding and giggling. The ax added its notes to the jumble of sounds as one of the men split firewood for the coming night. It seemed so peaceful that nothing could alter the forever-feel of the air. But the warm weather had brought tension too: Indian war parties seemed to come with the warm weather.

As Rachel ran to meet her brother she saw him look as a movement caught his eye. Then there were Indians everywhere. Her brother died with an expression of confusion on his face. She screamed as a painted warrior ran past her toward the cabin. Another came right at her. The field that had been so peaceful seemed to come alive with dozens of glistening and painted blurs, who rushed through the open gate toward the cabins.

Rachel's father barely had time to see the warrior who had just killed his son when a 72-caliber lead ball tore into his chest. Still outside, Rachel couldn't move. She saw and heard, but her legs refused to obey her command to try to help the fallen or to escape. She heard the screams of women and yells of men, along with war cries of the Indians. She could not drown out the sounds of metal and wood impacting with human flesh. Men and women fought for their lives in the haze and horror that burned up every sign of peace and tranquility.

A blow to the head knocked Rachel to the ground where she lay bleeding and dazed. The warrior left her for dead and went in pursuit of other children. The warrior did not know her strength. she crawled to the stacks of firewood and pulled the drying slabs of split wood down around and over her. The poverty that kept her family from having colorful clothing helped hide her as the grey skirt and faded brown shirt blended with the soft tones of sun-bleached wood. The screams continued all around her. She felt ashamed of hiding. Gunshots. More gunshots. Then she closed her eyes and huddled down into the wood, holding her hand and a part of her dress over her head wound trying to stem the flow of blood. The bright red of her blood was the only spot of color in her hiding place. She fervently wished she could close her ears, as she had closed her eyes, to stop the sounds of death around her. She prayed to God in heaven to stop these things from happening.

As the noise diminished, she realized it was death and not miracles that caused the screams to stop. She opened her eyes for a moment but the horror continued. Through a gap in the heap of firewood she watched an Indian, painted yellow and green, carefully peel the skin and hair from the head of one of her friends. Little Phillip had been smaller and younger than she was. He would never get older. It didn't make sense. Once again she shut her eyes tightly and refused to see, hear, or feel any more of this nightmare. The red eye of the sun slowly dipped behind the blue mountains as if it too had seen enough.

Gunshots. Gunshots always took her mind back to that day. Ten years was not enough to erase it. Somehow she knew a hundred would not be enough.

• • •

The squirming of the puppy brought Rachel back to the present and she saw her husband. He had shot his rifle at a target and was beginning to reload. He wore a breech cloth and leggings along with a stained shirt girdled by his leather work apron. Such clothing would look odd anywhere else on earth, but not here in the backwoods. Here things had to be practical first. And cheap. The gun in his hands was a most valuable tool, worth almost as much as everything in their crude log house. A gun maker and Indian trader, John had been trying to sight in a gun he had just finished. He was adding a few grains of blackpowder to the flintlock. She took resolute steps toward him.

John was turning toward Rachel's footsteps just as she came up to him. Before he knew it she'd shoved him hard. It was all he could do to stay on his feet.

"What the...?"

He was interrupted by Rachel. "Next time you shoot, you tell me...I thought it was Indians..." Rachel turned to walk away from him. John groaned. He'd forgotten.

"Are you alright?"

She ignored his question and continued to walk back to the cabin.

"Rachel?"

She stopped and turned to face him, barely controlling the tears that threatened to surface and said, "You scared me...and...I'm...we...are about to have a baby!"

13

John's confusion showed on his face. "You're what? What was that last part you said?"

"John. We're going to have a baby."

John looked intently at her, trying to understand the meaning of her words. She could see the comprehension building in his face. Then a little grin pulled his handsome lips into a smile as he looked into her eyes. He raised the new rifle toward the sky with one hand. Little carved curls and leaves that decorated the gunstock caught the light and cast their delicate shadows as John quietly said, "Rachel, I'm going to shoot."

He was exultant as he pulled the trigger. With a loud roar white smoke erupted from the gun and the freshly loaded roundball was sent into the heavens, clipping a dead branch at the top of a tall poplar tree on its way up. The excitement of the new baby seemed to be more than a single loud noise could celebrate, so John started yelling at the top of his lungs and did an Indian dance around Rachel. She giggled and laughed at his antics as the threatening tears of hurt became tears of joy. John dropped the gun to the ground, took Rachel in his arms and carried her into the cabin. Both were laughing and acting like kids. No one noticed but the chickens, and they didn't care. After the cabin door closed and it was a long time before Johns giggles and Rachel's squeals quieted down. Then even the quiet seemed to fade to a greater silence as darkness closed on the peaceful homestead. The new rifle lay forgotten as the chickens went to roost.

CHAPTER THREE

Early the next morning John had retrieved the rifle and sat in front of the fire, rubbing another layer of finish on the curly grain of the maple stock. The momma dog, Lizzy, was stretched out on the hearth. Rachel was still sleeping in the couple's beautiful four-poster bed. The burnished wood contrasted sharply with the rough walls of the log cabin. John had made it. He'd carved it like he would a rifle, and polished it for weeks, but Johns eyes and heart told him it was the girl it cradled that made the bed so beautiful.

John was deep in thought about the direction their lives were about to take with the arrival of their first child. The only family he had known since his parents died was an old man named Dobbs, who had taken him into his home when he was a boy. John had been apprenticed as a gunstock maker to Master Dobbs near Allentown, Pennsylvania. John knew he had relatives somewhere near Montrose, Scotland, and he had memories of a warm kitchen which always smelled of fresh bread, but the memories were very dim. He did not know anything about family life that did not depend on a business contract and servitude.

He was only five when his parents agreed that he was to work for Dobbs, a stranger. Their own indentured time had nearly been completed when a sickness struck and took his parents. If he had not been living with Master Dobbs at the time, John would have been carried away as well. John finished his apprenticeship when he was 17, and gave in to an overwhelming desire to see what the frontier was like.

He took to the frontier as natural as a fish takes to water. Before he met Rachel, John spent his life trading and living among the Indians. He returned to this crude cabin when winter closed the trading down, and built guns in one end while living in the other. This ability to build and work on guns gave him a good living. Better than most.

Rachel stirred in the bed and propped herself up to look at John. Her movement brought him out of his reverie. He said, "You should take it easy today. Don't be trying to keep up."

"You don't have to worry about me."

He put a serious expression on his tan face as he looked into her eyes. "Don't go feeling too special. I take care of all my good mares when they're with foal." The fake seriousness broke down as he said, "I'm also thinking of that little stallion you carry."

"Oh! It's a boy, is it?"

She got out of bed and walked over to John, kissed him, and stroked his face with her hand. "I guess I could stand to look at another handsome trader like the one I've got."

John grinned self-consciously. Twirling like a little girl Rachel crossed the rough-hewn floor and evicted the momma dog from her place on the hearth, then put a kettle of water on to boil. The dog walked to the door and looked back at John as if to beg him to open the door for the sake of her bladder. John put down the rifle he had been rubbing, and walked over to the door. He took a smoothbore gun from above the door before opening it to let the dog out. Then he closed the door behind Lizzy and listened to see if she reacted to any danger. After a moment, when he heard no barking or growling, he opened the door and looked outside. He could see Lizzy was busy giving breakfast to her oversized pups. Satisfied that no danger was near, he returned his bigbore gun to its place over the door. Then he went back to his chair by the fire and continued rubbing the finish on the new gun.

After a few moments he said, "We'll put the roof on the gun shop tomorrow if we get the rafters up today. Joshua is supposed to be coming by. It's a long trip for him and it's been a while since he's been here. I suppose there will be some others along too. I'm sure Josh will stop by the fort, so no telling who will show up. I wish I had told Josh to pick up some nails at the fort. As it is, he won't bring any, so I may need you to fetch 'em."

Rachel took a few brown eggs from a basket. "Maybe I could visit Catherine too, and get some things from Tom's store."

Just then the unlatched door was invaded by the pups who had finished their breakfast. They came into the room fighting awkwardly, tripping on one another. Rachel shooed the puppies out of the room. "Out you go! Go on, go on, you had your breakfast. We'll have little puddles everywhere if you stay in here." Rachel laid a board across the door to stop the return of the fuzzy hoard. Then she noticed that John was holding one of the pups. His back was to her and she savored the moment as she watched his gentleness with the puppy. She finally took the pup from him and put the rifle back in his hands.

"If you rubbed those guns half as much as you do the pups, it wouldn't take any time to get a finish on them." Rachel put the pup outside, then turned to ask John a question.

"John, can we....?" then she hesitated.

"Can we what?"

"Let's give one of these pups to Joshua. You know how partial he is to hunting dogs. It's been a year now since he lost his old Ben."

"Joshua could use a good dog. Hard to survive without a dog. Yep! We'll do it. Little Ben there is the best of the lot."

"I think he'll like him, John."

"He'll be here today. You give him to Josh. It'll mean a lot to him - I know it will. He needs a dog to watch his back."

CHAPTER FOUR

Same day in the forest;

Across the tall ridges a hunter rode quietly. Joshua wasn't far from John's homestead, but when life moved only as fast as a horse, it was far enough. The sounds of birds and insects were heard as a breeze moved through the leaves of the trees. The sound of two horses, and a voice half singing, half humming was lost in the soft air. The sounds were so quiet that the wings of birds and songs of insects hid them even from the ears of deer and squirrels. Joshua moved through the forest riding one horse and leading a pack horse loaded with a freshly killed deer.

Joshua's leggings, quilled moccasins, breech clout, and hunting shirt, had seen more than one season. Grease stains were evidence of many meals cooked and eaten over camp fires. His shirt was belted with an Indian burden strap, providing a sash with colorful designs woven into it. He knew it was special. Its great length was wrapped several times around the wearer's waist and tied at the back. Joshua had a tomahawk and knife stuck in the burden strap, and a small clay pipe in a warrior's knife bag hung around his neck. Tattoos on his thighs, arms and face, were a record that he had spent his childhood with the Catawba tribe. He was a man between worlds; unfit for civilized life, but born white. The creases on his face indicated a man with a good sense of humor who was quickly approaching middle age. Joshua would have been the first to admit he was starting to feel the effects of years of sleeping on the ground.

Suddenly Joshua stopped his singing and humming. He'd seen movement in a thicket a short distance away. It was a big buck deer. Joshua pulled his horse to a stop. The buck snorted but didn't run. Joshua, still mounted, slowly pulled his rifle up into position and fired. The riding horse tightened up but stayed put. The packhorse, however, threw her head back, bucked a couple of times at the roar of the rifle, and then ran away.

Joshua reached forward and patted his riding horse. "Well, at least you act like you have good sense." He looked toward the still departing packhorse, and said, "...And it looks like Georgina's still a little shy about guns."

Joshua eased out of the handmade wooden saddle and walked toward the fallen deer, reloading as he walked. As he approached, he saw that the death tremors had already stopped, and he paused to finish pouring a charge of black powder down the muzzle. Pulling his ramrod from its thimbles he used it to push the patched fifty caliber roundball down the barrel and seat it on the powder charge. Joshua spit tobacco juice into the deer path. Beneath the sassafras leaf that caught his spit he saw a footprint.

Tracks, moccasin tracks.

These tracks were not a white man's barefeet nor a settler's crude moccasin tracks either. Speaking in a low tone to his horse, he said, "It's Indian tracks. Shouldn't be none of those around here." Tugging on the horse's reins he said, "Come on. Ol' Josh smells trouble." Still mumbling to himself, he replaced the ramrod in its brass thimbles and primed the pan of his flintlock rifle.

"Every time I spit, I spit in a track belonging to a war party. I'd give up chewing if it wasn't so good for me." He paused a moment to look into the horse's large brown eye. Still muttering to his horse he mounted and rode off looking for Georgina. Joshua spit tobacco juice again, wishing these tracks weren't so close to the fort. As he rode, Joshua's eyes searched the forest; noting every shadow and every movement, turning his ears and nose to the wind making sure the way was clear.

He found Georgina grazing in a grassy clearing and dismounted to check the packsaddle on her back. He found the front saddle tree fork had loosened due to the banging it got during the packhorse's escape. He decided it would be fine until he could get Nemesis to tighten it for him at the fort. He remounted to return for the buck, mumbling to Georgina about how he should leave her to be butchered by the Indians, or how he should sell her to a farmer so she would have to work every day pulling a plow.

Joshua soon had the fresh-killed buck fastened alongside the one he shot earlier and headed to the fort. Even though the world looked beautiful, he felt a coldness in the summer air.

• • •

Kitcheogeemaw, eyes moving, tried to locate the direction of the very faint shot he had heard a short while before. One shot is hard to place, but two shots are hard to hide; but there was only one. Satisfied that it did not involve the safety of his party, he turned to face the warriors. They were packing away extra gear. He checked his flint and re-primed his gun before moving to another warrior and adding his own paint to the warrior's face. He tied a tiny bundle around his neck. He chanted something unintelligible to the man as he administered his protective medicine. These were rituals of war. Another warrior held a small mirror and freshened the war paint already on his face. Paint was important.

All were watchful. They knew that when they took their places they might have to lie still for many hours or even days until the moment of attack. A guard warrior, who was a good distance away, turned for a brief glance at his friends. Over his shoulder the Phares' homestead could be seen.

CHAPTER FIVE

Joshua splashed across Evitts Creek and approached Tom's Station. It was an average frontier fort, built strictly as a defense against small arms attack. Several raw cabins made an enclosure, with upright poles or posts connecting one cabin with another. Inside was a place big enough for the livestock and for people. Tom's Station was located a few miles south of Fort Cumberland. To the west the Potomac River could be traced by the gap it made between tall trees. It smelled like fish.

In and around the palisades, horses searched the overeaten pasture for a nibble of green. A few wagons, a cart, and farm tools, languished in the open or lay barely protected beneath crude shelters. People were walking towards work that needed done, or toward food that needed eating. A hammer on an anvil was heard over at the blacksmith shop. Children were playing.

The children spotted Joshua as he entered the gate and they began shouting his name with excitement. Joshua teased them as they clamored to be noticed. He stopped his horse for their safety. They pulled at his leggings for attention as he swung down from the horse. One child attempted to climb his leg. Joshua brushed little hands away as he said, "Mosquitos are bad today," He grabbed a little girl and pulled her up into his arms and tickled her pudgy little stomach and said, "This one feels like a tick!"

"I ain't no tick!"

Joshua said, "What! Well surely you ain't! What are you then?

"I'm a little girl!"

"What? ...Children!?... Bashaw, worse than bugs!" As he set the little girl down he removed a coin from his belt bag and flipped it to the children. He said, "You young-ins go on, get ya some cone sugar. I'll be over fer mine in a little while."

When they were gone, one child remained, waiting to be noticed. Lewis Hughes had been orphaned. He hid during an Indian attack and when the smoke cleared he was the only one left alive. Miles from any neighbors he had starved for days until Joshua had found him sitting in the field next to the cabin trying to gnaw a few kernels from an ear of flint corn. The child had attached himself to Joshua since that day. Three years later the boy still kept watch for Joshua. While other children played, Lewis watched and waited.

Lewis had been taken in by Tom Thomas and his wife Catherine, but as far as Lewis was concerned, Joshua was his family. He lived for the times when Joshua was at the fort and they could be together. Some day he and Joshua were going to go trading together; they were going to be partners forever.

"Joshua,"

The hunter looked at the boy and said, "Lewis! If you don't catch up to them, you'll miss out on those sweets."

"I want to stay here with you, Josh. Are we still going to see Mr. Phares and Rachel?"

"Sure are. I don't say things I don't mean. If you're gonna be here come help me with this deer, the other one is for the Phares'. We'll take it to them as soon as I get Nem to tighten the fork on this pack saddle... that rascally Georgina nearly busted it apart this morning. Must have hit it on a tree when she took off runnin'.

Lewis moved to help and saw the buck. The animal was massive. His confidence bolstered by the invitation to help, Lewis started to tease. "Where did you get this little ol' deer?", he said with all the seriousness a spindly child could muster.

"Way out on the...Hey, what do you mean LITTLE?"

Lewis spit, just like Joshua often did, and said, "Well, if that was a fish, I'd a throwed him back."

"Well you ornery..." Joshua grabbed Lewis and had a tickling scuffle with him. After a minute Joshua stopped, winded. "You're getting too big for me to handle, let's go see Nem and be on our way. We got a lot to do and a long way to go before this day is over."

Lewis and Joshua led the horse to the blacksmith shop brushing dirt and dust off their clothes. The blacksmith was Nemesis; a big, burly, very black man. He was wet with sweat in the dark shelter that protected the great bellows and heavy anvil, his dark skin reflected the blueness of the skyline or the golden green of grass outside. He was busy at the anvil, smoke and fire outlining a chest as solid as a tree, and near as big. Joshua motioned for

22

Lewis to be quiet, snuck up behind Nemesis, and leaned close to his ear. "If I was an injun, I'd had your scalp by now."

Nemesis jumped but didn't turn around. He finished the stroke that was interrupted, patiently putting up with Joshua's childishness. Nemesis laid the hammer down and turned slowly while wiping sweat out of his eyes, noticing Lewis who quietly moved to stand beside Joshua.

He spoke to Lewis from the heights of the smokey room. "Now, Lewis! How many times have I told you not to bring children around here?" Looking up at Joshua he continued, "Some of 'em ain't got no sense at all, no matter how old they get." With a grin spreading across his face he said, "How are you, Josh? I see you made it back."

"Fine, just fine. I'm going out to give John Phares a hand with his gun shop and thought I'd stop by to git Lewis and see how things are going with you."

"Well things are good here." Nemesis waited for a reply. There wasn't any. The two men just looked at each other happy to be near one another again...alive. Nem asked, "Well, do you need something or do you just want to make me miserable? I got things to do. I can't just ride around the country like you do."

"I do have something for you to do alright. Georgina busted my pack saddle, reckon you could patch it for me?"

Nemesis wiped his hands on his apron as he walked to Joshua's mare. He checked her saddle, pulling and twisting at the tree fork that had pulled loose from the bars, grunted and snorted, then the mare's hooves attracted his attention. After a another grunt or two he walked over to check the shoes on Joshua's riding horse. While he bent over the horse's hoof he looked up, noticing Joshua's belly.

"The shoes are worn bad. Maybe the load's gettin' to be too much for him."

"Why, you ol' skunk...you sure ain't missed no meals either that I can notice."

Nemesis dropped the hoof and stood up. "Give me half of the hour and I'll have it ready for you."

Joshua grabbed Lewis, slung him onto his shoulder and turned to leave. "I have to see Tom about a few things anyhow and I'll settle up with you then."

"You ain't got no money anyhow." Nemesis waved him on and went back to the forge.

Joshua hauled Lewis over to the storehouse and peered into the dark building. It was lighted only by the open door. The children and their sugar were long gone. Smells of tallow, tanned hides, hemp rope, tobacco and other trade goods were overwhelming after the fresh outside air. Putting Lewis down to stand on his own two feet Joshua yelled, "TOM!"

"Josh, is that you?"

Tom was a crusty old timer on the frontier. He had obtained a King's deed to this land in 1739 when there were only Indians living here. He had to make a treaty with them in order to occupy the land. He was one of the white men who understood the red man. At this place He was the militia captain, storekeeper, farm manager, and news keeper. Joshua and Tom gripped each other's hands in greeting.

"Cap'n Tom, how are you?"

"Well, I feel more like I do now than I did a while ago. How you holdn' up, Josh? What brings you in today? I didn't expect to see you for a while."

"I'm going out to help John Phares do some work on his new shop. Since he and Rachel got married, he don't have the room in that cabin he once had. I told him last fall that I'd drop by in the spring to give him a hand. He licked his lips. I'm going to get some good home cooking from Rachel too!"

Tom began to remember the news from that end of the woods. "That's right. Lewis has been acting like a worm on a hot brick since the weather broke, waiting for you to show up so he could go off with you. Maybe me and some of the boys will ride out this afternoon and we'll get that gun shop done in prime fashion." Tom pointed toward the deer hanging out of the reach of half a dozen dogs. "I saw when you came in the gate that you have plenty of meat for a good cabin raisin'."

Joshua leaned over to Lewis, who was stuffing his mouth with the piece of rock candy he had selected, and said, "Lewis, go check and see if Nemesis needs help, and tell him I'll be along in a minute or two." Lewis nodded his head and ran out the door.

When Lewis was gone, Joshua leaned forward. "Tom, I think we got trouble...Maybe nothing...but...."

"What's wrong?"

"I seen tracks, six, maybe eight men...maybe a war party. The tracks were as much as a day old...no older, and look to be Wyandot...maybe Miami, but I think Wyandot."

Tom's eyebrows furrowed. "A war party... We better send word. I don't want to take any chances."

Joshua appreciated Tom's calmness. "Tom, you know, they might even be friendly, just being careful."

Tom moved out from behind the counter now, to stand beside Joshua. After thinking a moment, he said, "I reckon I'll still put some spies out this afternoon."

"That ain't a bad idea...but we can't quit living for the fear of dying."

The two men shook hands. Joshua started to walk out the door and Tom stopped him. "Josh, you forgot your supplies."

"You're right. Just give me a plug of that tobacco now and I'll pick up the rest of what I need when I pass back through here in a couple of days. . . And we'll figure out how much credit I got left from last year's furs...And can I have a piece of that rock sugar?"

Tom smiled and handed over the tobacco and sugar. Joshua put the tobacco in his haversack and walked out munching on the compacted brown sugar. He watched Joshua walk into the daylight then moved through the shadows of his store to his rifle, powder horn, shooting bag and tomahawk. The gun was loaded, the hatchet was sharp. Tom expected his son Michael any time; he would feel a lot better when he arrived.

Nemesis and Lewis were deep in conversation when Joshua approached. Nemesis looked and said, "I just finished." Joshua asked how much he owed.

"A leg off that other deer would be plenty."

They shook hands and Joshua said, "I thank you for getting this done so fast. Maybe we'll see you out at the Phares' place?"

Yeah, I'm thinking so.

A short time later Joshua mounted his horse and reached down and grabbed Lewis' outstretched hand to swing him up behind him. They said their goodbyes to Nem, and the man and boy started out the fort gate. They rode north in the direction of Fort Cumberland. John and Rachel lived along Evitts Creek about half way between Tom's Station and Fort Cumberland. They would be there soon.

CHAPTER SIX

As Joshua and Lewis rode through the southern foothills of Warrior Mountain they could still smell the river on the east wind. Lewis rode behind the hunter as Joshua sang and pointed to various trees and plants. He was quizzing Lewis about the woods.

"What kind of tree is that?"

Lewis responded, "Poplar."

"What's the bark good for?"

"Head pains," said Lewis

"Thata boy!" Now, what is that plant with the pointy leaves?"

"Smart Weed," said Lewis

"Yep, what's it good for?"

After a few moments, Lewis said, "I forget."

"You'll wish you hadn't forgot if you get cut and it goes bad; them leaves kills the poison."

"I'll remember, Josh."

Joshua grabbed Lewis's knee affectionately. "I know you will."

Lewis hugged onto Joshua and laid his head against his back. Joshua's heart was full of contentment and he began to sing again. The sounds of the horses and the singing of the rider slowly faded as the forest swallowed them from sight. Two jay birds were fighting over the possession of a tree limb, and the rat-tat-tat of a woodpecker feeding on hatchling bugs under the bark of a dead tree covered the singing like one music note covers the sound of another.

• • •

Rachel was sitting at the front of the cabin enjoying the peace and quiet of her homestead. She hummed a little and then sang a word or two of a song that lingered in her mind. She was waiting for the cooking to get done. John was chopping wood again. There was always wood to be split.

Suddenly Rachel realized that John's attention had shifted from chopping wood to the edge of the forest. Riders were coming. Rachel walked over to John and took his arm so they could watch together.

Rachel liked how John got excited when his friends came to visit. He reminded her of one of the puppy's. "Here comes Joshua," said John, "and he's got Lewis with him".

Momma dog ran barking past them toward Joshua and Lewis to greet them with tail wagging. As the riders got within shouting distance, Joshua yelled, "Hello the house. Hello John Phares…I reckon this is a right good day for puttin' up a gun shop."

Joshua rode up to a large flat stump at the front of the cabin and stopped. He saw the good tableware Rachel had set out on the stump in preparation for their meal. He pawed beard stubble on his face and appeared to have eyes only for the food.

"I could use a bite to eat first"

When Lewis was lowered to the ground he ran over to the pups which were running and falling over each other.

"Well, I hope you brought an appetite!' said John. "Nice deer you have! You've been busy on the way in!"

"I figured you could use some fresh meat, bein' busy an' all…if everyone shows, we'll be lickin' the bones."

Joshua spit, then dismounted. Arms extended, he and John bear-hugged one another, and pounded each other, almost starting to wrestle. Rachel cleared her throat, and the two men turned slightly in her direction. A smile started on Rachel's face. Joshua moved toward Rachel, took his hat off and shyly hugged her as though he was afraid of breaking her or getting her dirty.

John said, "Let's tend these horses and get this deer skinned, food's almost ready!"

They walked the horses to the shed, Joshua pounding John on the back, purely happy to be together, bragging about the gun John had made him, and how it shot dead center.

Rachel listened as their voices moved away and faded beneath the sounds of Lizzy's panting "You did a fine job on that gun, John. When the deer see it they just fall down and give up the ghost; they know it's no use to fight it…when ol' Tussey speaks, the meat's in the pot!" said Joshua. She smiled.

I made something for Lewis," said John. Joshua tied the horses to the chestnut rail fence beside the open-faced shed that John had been using as a temporary gun shop and followed John inside. John reached up under the joists and pulled out a toy replica of Joshua's gun. When Joshua saw the toy gun, he said, "Well, it's just like ol' Tussy. That shines, he'll really like it! Can we give it to him now?"

Josh didn't wait for an answer and headed to find Lewis. John followed.

Enjoying the moment, he grinned as he watched Joshua give the gun to Lewis. Maybe this was what having a family felt like. He didn't know who was more excited - Josh or Lewis. But John knew all the work he put into making the toy gun was worth it when he saw the look on their faces.

They were soon sitting around the stump eating. Lewis was nearby with the new toy gun on his lap. Puppies were frolicking around and over him as he tried to eat and play with his gun and the pups at the same time.

Joshua said, "That boy is as near heaven as he'll be in this lifetime…dogs… guns…. food… it's what boy-dreams are made of." Rachel asked if anyone wanted more to eat. The men told her what a fine meal it was and that they couldn't hold another bite. John excused himself. "I'll be right out, Josh, I want to get my pipe. Can I get you one?" Joshua reached for his own pipe in his neck bag and told John not to get any tobacco as he just bought some fresh from Tom. The men filled and lit their pipes, and relaxed in the serenity only the company of dear friends can bring.

Joshua and John had spent many years together. Both men had traded and trapped over hundreds of miles of uncharted country. The time they had spent together had given each an understanding of the other that few people experience. Each man's life had depended on the other many times. The whole mixture of each man could be sensed by the other.

"Something wrong, John?"

"I don't know…I feel it more than I know it…You see any sign?" Joshua started to speak but was interrupted by a "Hello" that was yelled from the far end of the open field.

Everyone stood and looked in the direction of the sound to see who was coming.

Tom, his son Michael, and Nemesis were riding across the field toward them. The blue haze of the Appalachian Mountains behind them framed the confident motions of the men. At this distance the bulk and size of Nemisis distinguished him from the others. As they watched the forms of the men become clear and sharp Lewis came running with his new gun, followed by the string of puppies. The boy ran to Nemesis as he was getting off his horse.

"Look at my gun, Nem, look at my gun!"

The big man graciously took time to admire the fine toy while the rest greeted each other with hand shaking and back slapping. Visitors didn't come everyday in the back-country. Even Lewis was caught up with chattering to Nemesis. Forgetting that it had only been a few hours since he had seen him, Lewis said, "Come on, I'll show you big guns John is making. Wait till I'm bigger. I'm going to get one. Come on, Nem, come on!" The child grabbed a big thick finger and pulled the giant black man away from the others. Nemesis liked the boy. Most of the time the child was somber and shy. The boy's quiet, controlled sadness reminded him of his own children.

Nemesis had a family but they were owned by a man who lived on the western edge of Baltimore. The big man's dream was to save enough money to buy his wife and children. It was difficult to find hard money in these mountains. No one had much. Barter was the backbone of the backwoods economy, so Nemesis learned how to carry out sophisticated and complex trades that could turn a haunch of deer meat into hard money. He was almost there. He would tell no one how much hard money he had saved because he was savvy enough to know that jealousy would rear its ugly head if the poor people around him knew how much he had stashed away. The big man had been brought to western Maryland by the son of the people who owned his wife. The son had some bad luck and lost everything he owned when he tried a crossing the Allegheny River on a raft. That was the first time Nemesis met Tom. Tom was the surveyor of Prince George's County, Maryland, at the time and was involved in surveying a road to the Allegheny River, reporting on the location of Indian settlements, who they traded with, the quality of the soil, courses and locations of streams and rivers, and any other information of benefit to the Ohio Company and the Colony of Maryland. Needing new supplies, the inexperienced newcomer tried to talk credit but Tom insisted on cash or trade. When the dealing was over Nemesis belonged to Tom. Tom, always a rebel of the most consistent kind, wrote out papers to make him free. Tom was an odd man that way. Once Tom was involved with establishing the proper place for the Pennsylvania and Maryland border line. Captured and arrested by the opposing party, who tried to drown him as they crossed the Susquehanna River, he was hauled to Philadelphia. Tom, refused to be intimidated and pronounced Philadelphia the loveliest city in... Maryland. Nemesis was free because Tom was so stubborn and loyal to his own mind. To Tom's way of thinking all men were born free by right and the writing of papers didn't do anything but state the obvious. Nemesis was grateful to Tom, but not because he made him free. It was because he respected him both before and after he wrote the papers.

Lewis moved into the lean-to gun shop with Nemesis. He had let go of the finger, but let Nem fold the slender pale hand deep into his iron-calloused palm. Nemesis breathed in the moment, thinking that maybe someone somewhere would care so carefully for his own children. They were so much alike, Lewis and his own children: They already knew things children shouldn't know; Lewis knew horror, Nem's children knew slavery.

After admiring Johns guns for the benefit of little Lewis, Nemesis stopped a moment to slice the back strap of a deer into several steaks and carried them to where John had struck a fire. The smell of roasting venison soon had mouths watering. Rachel swung the iron pot of new potatoes and small onions back over the fire and warmed the fresh baked corn bread that was left from earlier. Tom, Michael and Nemesis were soon stuffing themselves with food. When all felt they couldn't hold another bite, Rachel dug out the dutch oven she had buried in the coals. She had made an apple cobbler with the last of the dried apples she had saved for just such an occasion. This was topped with maple sugar and fresh spring house cream.

As Rachel started to clean up, Joshua saw she couldn't carry all the plates and cups, so he helped her. Indians would make fun of him for helping a woman, but Rachel knew better than to tease; she liked the help. As Joshua emerged from the cabin he saw Lizzy nursing her pups. Joshua missed his hunting dog. He and ol' Ben had traveled many miles together and this pup looked and acted just like his grand-pappy did when he was a pup. Joshua scratched behind the pup's ear and looked across the yard to watch Michael, Tom, and Nemesis prop up an two foot chunk of tree trunk for a target. He picked up the pup and walked over to see the fun.

John had taken a piece of charcoal from the fire and drawn a black mark across the grain of the target. Sticking a tomahawk was one point, cutting the edge of the black mark was three points, and splitting the black mark was five points. Every point was counted and marked down. Lewis and Rachel joined the men to watch.

While the others stepped up to the mark, John pulled Joshua aside to resume the conversation that had been interrupted by the arrival of Nem and the others.

"You've seen Indian sign haven't you Josh?"

"Yeah, but there has been no trouble around here."

John didn't like not being sure. He wagged a thumb toward Rachel and said, "I want Rachel to go to the big fort to get the nails. Maybe you could go along with her. If you see anything, I'd feel better if she were to stay there." Joshua agreed. A moment or two passed in silence. Then John said, "Josh, we're going to have a baby." He paused, then added, "A boy no doubt!"

"Well, that's the best news I' could hear!"

Rachel had turned in time to hear the last part of the conversation. She said to the two men, "You sure are going to be disappointed if it's a girl, and probably half the country too, as much as you two talk."

Joshua yelled the news to the tomahawk throwers. "We're going to have a baby! Uh...I mean John is...uh...Rachel and John is." The tomahawks stopped. Nemesis said, "Give this lady a seat...come on...why didn't you tell us sooner. Whoopy! A little baby! That's prime."

Rachel laughingly said, "It's alright, I feel fine. Anyway the dishes are done. You'll just get in my way. Besides, if you all ever get done playing, all of you should be busy puttin' up John's gun shop."

She was right. It was long past time to work. As they gathered their hatchets Rachel turned to Joshua and said, "Now... what were you and John saying about Indians?"

"Oh nothing...."

But Joshua knew she wouldn't settle for that so he thought he would tell her about his recent dream. "Well... I did have a dark and nasty dream..." Under his breath, "murdering savages..." Louder he said, "But it was just a dream."

John returned, and seeing the direction the conversation had taken, tried to change the subject. He said to Rachel, "Joshua's going with you to the fort to pick up the nails."

Rachel was not giving this up. She asked, "What was your dream, Joshua?"

Joshua hesitated, then answered, "It was a dark kind of a dream, yes sir...DARK, sleepin' on the ground must be getting' hard on me."

"Well, tell me!"

"Well, they killed me..." Then he laughed as if it was all a joke.

Rachel, horrified, said, "Maybe...maybe, we better just stay here, the gun shop can wait!"

Joshua smiled gently, "Naw...Now don't you get all frazzled...I don't believe in dreams nohow, especially ones where an ol' stag like me gets killed." Joshua pointed to the men standing there and said, "Besides, with these fellers around, there ain't going to be no trouble."

A quiet moment passed as each of one of them remembered their personal losses. But Rachel refused to let memories of death set the pace for a living moment. Seeing that she wasn't going to convince them to tell her anything she turned to Joshua, "John and me were talking and we know how much you loved your ol' Ben. Well, we figured maybe you would like to have one of his grandsons...maybe Lil' Ben here."

Joshua looked down at the little fur ball that lay almost asleep in his hands, and slowly lifted his eyes to meet theirs. His face hid all emotion, but his voice tightened a little as he said, "That shines...Purely shines . . ." Clearing his throat he tried to speak away the softness in himself that he considered weakness. "Ol' Ben...me and him spent many winters together. I just don't know how to thank you enough." Rachel and John smiled at each other. John reached over and petted Lil' Ben.

Tom finally broke the mood and said, "If we don't get started on the walls of that gun shop, we won't be ready for those nails when you do get back with them. It ain't building itself, come on grab an ax and let's get to work." The men stacked their guns, hunting bags and horns against the stump that had served as an eating table. Keeping guns handy was old habit even when there seemed to be no need for caution. One of John's horses was soon in harness pulling the logs up from the edge of the woods where John had several trees down, de-limbed, and the bark off. Tom and Nemesis were notching each end of the logs and preparing to set them in place with the help of another horse, a harness and strong rope.

Rachel went to the cabin to get her things together for the ride to the fort. When she came back outside, she called to John that she was ready to leave.

Joshua wasn't going anywhere without his new pup, so he picked up Lil' Ben and put the pup into the fold of his hunting shirt. Then he patted Lizzy, and told her, "Don't worry, I'll take good care of him ol' girl." Then he mounted his horse, asking Michael to hand up his gun, Ol' Tussy, while he adjusted his possibles bag and horn. Joshua rested his rifle across the pommel of his saddle in such a way that it could be used in an instant if needed.

Rachel had changed into a clean dress, fixed her hair, and was now wearing shoes. John took her hand to see her off and said, "Mrs. Phares! I'm not sure I should let you go away from here looking as pretty as you do."

Joshua agreed. "You sure do clean up nice"

Rachel, acting formal, said, "Thank you, thank you both."

Lewis led Rachel's horse over to the couple and handed the reins to John. John turned back to Rachel, put his arms around her and they looked into each other's eyes.

Joshua said, "Well…haul off and kiss her if you're gonna, we ain't got all day ya know."

Joshua was petting his pup as it stuck its head out of the folds of his shirt watching the lovers. John and Rachel kissed as Joshua said to Lil' Ben, "Just like love sick pups…no offense, Ben."

John and Rachel gave each other a final hug and John said something quietly in Rachel's ear and she responded, "Alright, John…I will." She whispered "I love you."

John lifted her onto the horse. He took hold of her hand for a few seconds even as the horse stepped away. He followed until the increasing speed of the horse pulled them apart. Rachel looked back at John briefly, then turned away as they entered the shade of forest. John's eyes followed Rachel until she blended with the shadows.

CHAPTER SEVEN

Ambush

Joshua started singing as they approached the forest. A bear was almost surprised as it dug for roots. It was the fault of the squirrels that scolded so noisily. The bear saw them and slipped into the thicket far more quietly than seemed possible. A deer lifted its head and turned to investigate, then it also turned and ran.

Rachel was thinking that if the nails were at the fort as promised, she would be able to get her supplies then visit with some friends. She and Joshua would be able to return first thing in the morning. John's gun shop would be finished tomorrow. Her thoughts were light and happy as she enjoyed the ride. She started humming along with Joshua as he continued his song. A thought crossed her mind and she asked, "Joshua, were you singing in your dream when they killed you?"

He didn't respond but after he sang a few more notes, he shut right up. Rachel was sorry she had blurted out her thoughts before she realized what she was saying. It seemed to have clouded their sunny day. Joshua seemed to be very alert. Something felt very wrong. Even the horses were nervous. Joshua started to say something, then stopped. He realized, too late, that they were already in the middle of big trouble.

In the blink of an eye, Rachel's horse was hit by a large caliber lead rifle ball and her horse started to go down. Rachel screamed, "Joshua!!" She was knocked unconscious in the fall. She did not move. Joshua thought she was dead.

He faced her killers as an arrow hit him in the leg and a load of buckshot struck his lower back, knocking him from his horse. Another arrow stabbed his upper leg. Then another. Small shot hit Joshua's horse. It went wild with pain and fear, throwing clumps of root and dirt into the air as it broke away, terrified. Joshua's pup was sent rolling as the hunter hit the ground. Joshua groaned as the arrows protruding from his body broke in the fall and twisted deeper into his flesh. Lil' Ben scampered deep into the brush and looked back at what was going on.

With broken arrow shafts projecting from his legs Josh regained his feet. Looking at his gun, he saw that it was broken in half at the wrist. Concerned for Rachel he turned to see human forms that moved like ghosts. They were almost to her. When he saw Rachel laying helpless in front of them he forgot everything; he forgot he was wounded; he forgot his gun was broken; he forgot he was only one man against many; he forgot his dark dream; and ran to attack.

He was met by more painted ghosts who emerged from the woods. He ran as best he could toward a warrior with a tomahawk, and clubbed him with the gun barrel. He knew it was a good hit so he then turned to meet another warrior from a different direction. Joshua shoved the jagged wrist of the broken gun into the warrior's chest like a spear, taking him off his feet. Another arrow hit Joshua at nearly the same instant a gunshot knocked him down. Another arrow pierced his stomach. Another. Then another. Blood poured out of his mouth. He was growing weaker, almost helpless.

Joshua now rolled and used his arms to push himself upright on the ground because his stomach muscles did not work. A warrior painted Yellow and green grabbed him by his hair. Joshua looked Yellow-Hand in the eyes but had no way to defend himself, he could not move. Blood spilled out upon the ground and filled his stomach. He could do nothing else so he spit a mouthful of his own blood all over the warrior. Enraged at this act, the yellow Indian scalped the helpless Joshua and watched him closely as he died. Too weak to move, Joshua could only see the branches above him. He noticed black powder smoke from Indian guns weaving upward through a thousand leaves. More arrows thudded into his body but he couldn't feel them anymore: he was drifting through the leaves with gun smoke . . . on his way to heaven.

· · ·

The sound of the first gunshot was barely heard by the workers at the Phares homestead. It sounded like a puff of breath. but it was heard. At the sound of the second shot, which was almost instantaneous, John dropped the ax he was using and ran for his gun. The other men looked at each other as John, running hard, screamed, "RACHEL!!!!!"

John snatched the new rifle as he ran by the stump. He did not take time to unhitch his horse; drawing his knife he slashed the reins short, leaped on its back and raced toward the sound of the gunshots. Tom and Michael ran to catch their horses. Lewis was wide eyed, saying nothing as a tear ran down his cheek, his little toy gun was tight in his hands. He had been through this before.

· · ·

Rachel was coming to her senses and getting her focus as Joshua's killer, Yellow-Hand, straddled Joshua's lifeless body and finished by wiping his knife on Joshua's shirt. He turned to see Rachel watching in horror, her eyes focused on Joshua. Rachel knew death did strange things to people. Death made them strangers. That man on the ground could not be Joshua; that man was dead, but Joshua was always so alive. Power went away from her every muscle when she realized Yellow-Hand was approaching her. Yellow-Hand reached for Rachel but stopped as Kitcheogeemaw stepped between them. Kitcheogeemaw gave an order. The other warriors grabbed Joshua's gear and assisted the wounded warrior that Joshua had speared with the broken gun. They started to move out. There was no hesitation.

Yellow-Hand looked at Kitcheogeemaw, then at Rachel, then quickly moved off. The guard warrior pulled Rachel's horse to its feet. Rachel was surprised. She thought the horse had been killed. There was only a little blood above the withers of the animal and the horse looked strong as ever. She had heard about "creasing" but this was the first time she saw it. She always heard that Indians could temporarily stun a horse by barley wounding it at the neck. Now she knew for certain. The warrior brought the horse to Kitcheogeemaw, who checked the horse's wound, then loaded Rachel. Quickly they departed.

· · ·

John was breathing hard and wet with sweat from his frantic run even before entered the forest. He had not gone far beyond the treeline when he saw Joshua's terrified riding horse pounding toward him. He had to turn his horse aside to avoid the wounded horse as it passed him terrified and bleeding. John only glanced as it made its way back to the homestead before he whipped his horse back into the path toward Rachel. The forest was a blur as he pounded through the trees. He rode past the familiar old chestnut tree, then past the first turn. On he went as hard as he could ride. Evitts Creek was just a stone's throw away when he saw Joshua's body.

John leaped from the back of his horse and approached the clearing where Joshua was lying. Looking at every tree and shadow that could conceal an enemy, his nerves he read the signs left by the savage attackers.

John stopped still in his tracks; he didn't even breathe as he turned toward the sound he heard. He could not understand what it could be. At last a whine told John it was the puppy. John stepped carefully and reached for Little Ben then held him close as he continued to search in vain to find his wife. She was gone.

He walked to Joshua and knelt down next to him. Tears of frustration fell onto the fur of the confused puppy. John felt as though his heart had been torn from his breast. In his despair, John prayed. "She's took...Please...Not...." A sob choked him. When he could breathe again he prayed in a more formal and audible tone, "Dear God, watch over her...keep her...." His voice trailed off and became silent. Then he began to circle so he could find the tracks that would tell him what direction the war party had taken.

As he circled, Tom and Michael rode up and dismounted. Knowing better than to disturb the tracks until the story they told was well read they stood still to wait for John. John continued to pray and search for signs of what had happened. With a few motions John directed them to make a larger circle to look for any sign that may help them determine how many Indians were involved, how experienced or dangerous they were. They widened their search just to make sure Rachel had not ran from them...or lay dead in the thickets. They looked for anything that would help discover...or recover Rachel. John had read the tracks: A fallen horse, the print of Rachel's body, no wound, no blood, then the horse pushed to its feet and Rachel's footprints disappear into the confusion of all the rest. It would take time to sort the trails and get on the right track.

Tom and Michael approached John. Quietly Tom said, "There are too many of them for us. We'll get help and follow." Michael put his hand on John's shoulder and said, "Don't worry, John. We'll get her back."

The sound of an approaching horse was heard and all three men moved to step out of sight before they realized that it was Nemesis - with Lewis riding behind him. Before anyone could stop him, Lewis was off the horse and running to Joshua. Nemesis could not have known that Joshua lay dead. He would not have believed his friend could be killed at all. But Lewis saw his friend, and ran to him before Nemesis knew it. The boy stopped at Joshua's feet as though he had run into a wall. No sound came from him. Nem reached the boy and lifted him away but already a change had come over the boy. He did not cry like a child. The boy only stared dry-eyed toward Joshua as Nemesis tried to block the awful sight with his body.

As Nemesis stood with him, the men laid Joshua across the saddle of Tom's horse. They agreed it would be best to head back to John's cabin and pick up whatever supplies and equipment they would need. Then they would come back and pick up the tracks of the war party. It wouldn't take long and they would be ready to stay out several days if they had to. The tracks seemed to be heading South but they would likely turn West, which would bring them near Fort Cumberland. They could pick up some more men there and be after Rachel at first light.

John didn't argue. He had been on other rescue attempts and knew that a fight too soon after the capture would almost certainly insure Rachel's death. When Indians were pursued and feared being caught, they would tomahawk and scalp their prisoners rather than let them be recovered.

CHAPTER EIGHT

Lewis had not said a word since he saw Joshua covered tightly in a blanket in preparation for burial. It was a burial that must be done by others under the directions of Tom's wife, Catherine. The men had to get moving quickly. As they gathered up their things Lewis sat on the front porch with his toy gun lying next to him, holding Little Ben, absent mindedly petting the puppy. John was torn between rushing wildly after Rachel and taking a few moments to comfort this devastated boy. With a struggle between impatience and compassion tearing him apart he sat down next to the boy and put his arm around him. Lewis looked up at John and said something that was to haunt John for a long time. "Everyone I love gets killed by Indians."

John knew the boy had no hope. John did. In spite of everything he hoped he would see Rachel again. Lewis was different. Death had made a prison in the child's mind: Death took people away and locked them away forever. They never came back. Lewis never knew to hope for a better end. He never knew to hope at all.

John pulled the boy close and said, "Little Ben didn't get took and he needs someone now that Josh is gone. Would you take him, Lewis? I know Joshua would want you to have Ben." Lewis didn't answer, but he held the pup closer to him.

John held the boy for a moment then continued to prepare. There was not much time for comfort. Extra food was put out for the dog, and livestock was turned out to graze. John had packed what little he needed to stay on the trail, and the men were soon headed toward Fort Cumberland, where Lewis would be safe.

CHAPTER NINE

Miles north of Evitt's Creek the sun was getting low in the horizon and the warm day was starting to cool. Rachel face was swollen and a blue bruise darkened the skin across her temple. Pain was starting to take its toll. She was mentally and physically exhausted.

Her horse was forced to move faster. A prisoner tie had been looped around her neck. Colorful porcupine quills that decorated it bit into her throat. Her hands were tied. Kitcheogeemaw saw she was having trouble balancing herself on the horse. He dropped back and untied her so she could sit upright. Still off balance, he steadied her, paused, then returned to his original position.

Rachel became more aware of of things around her with each mile they traveled. Heavily armed and painted, six men were running tirelessly. She studied the mean one she came to know as Yellow Hand. Joshua's graying, bloodied scalp hung from his belt. Rachel tried to control herself but she couldn't. She leaned to one side of her horse and threw up.

As the last bit of daylight was fading, Kitcheogeemaw signaled for his most experienced men to find a place to rest. He sent two scouts out to check their back trail. The group stopped beside a stream. One of the scouts returned and exchanged a few words with Kitcheogeemaw, then began to unpack small pouches of food. The younger fighters stood or squatted while the older warriors sat on the trunk of a fallen tree.

Kitcheogeemaw moved to Rachel and helped her down. One of the warriors tended to the wounded warrior, another took care of the horse. Rachel tried to get blood flowing in her legs. They were nearly numb from being tied on the horse for so many hours. She felt very sick again and fell to her knees. Her hand went instinctively to her belly. Yellow-Hand was watching. He watched as she held her belly. She didn't notice the mean one's eye on her. He walked toward her and pointed to her stomach and said, "Baby…?"

Rachel didn't answer, but her eyes betrayed her. Yellow-Hand knew she was with child. A smile began to break on the mean one's face. He pulled his knife and made several false jabs at her stomach, laughing all the while. He was playing. Rachel struggled to keep away from his advances with the knife and fell backward trying to keep distance between her and the warrior. Kitcheogeemaw was angered, and with a menacing tone in the Wyandot language, quietly said, "Enough…Yellow-Hand…enough!!!"

Kitcheogeemaw gave orders to everyone that she be left alone. Yellow-Hand grudgingly obliged. Kitcheogeemaw brought Rachel a blanket, and handed her a piece of jerked venison, which she refused by shaking her head and putting her face in her hands. Rachel was very near breaking down. Words that she and John had voiced every night came to her and she asked God's help in sustaining her through this. She knew she was not alone and that John was doing everything he could to rescue her; she just had to stand fast.

She gathered strength from these thoughts; she knew her best chance was to show no weakness. Rachel needed to be alert. she would try to remember every path, every stream, every landmark that she would see on this journey, so she could retrace her way home if she got away somehow.

It was almost dark and there would be no fire this night. Rachel was watching the Indians very closely now. A look of determination had replaced the fear that had shown on her face earlier. Yellow-Hand had made a small willow hoop and stretched Joshua's scalp on it. Rachel watched him scrape it, then comb the hair. The warrior saw that her attention was on his actions and he held the scalp so she could see it clearly and grinned at her discomfort. The Indians talked in low tones for a few minutes, gestures were made toward the direction they had come. The conversation ended and the Indians settled down for the night.

Kitcheogeemaw made signs for Rachel to wrap up in a blanket and lay down between him and another warrior. She obeyed the order without expression. Her hands were tied and the prisoner strap that had bound her earlier was tied around her neck and stretched out, one long tie on either side. Each man lay on an end of the strap. With any attempt to escape both warriors would be alerted by her movements.

Rachel lay awake for a long time thinking about what could happen to her, remembering stories told by other people who had escaped from the Indians, or those who had been released after months or years of captivity.

Rachel's feelings went from hope to despair many times before she silently cried herself to sleep that night.

. . .

Lewis was covered in a blanket, sleeping with Little Ben at the Ohio Company Trading Post across the Potomac from Wills Creek and Fort Cumberland. His toy gun lay close by. John, Tom, Michael and Nemesis were at Fort Cumberland trying to recruit men to help them rescue Rachel. Several men had volunteered and were quickly making moccasins. They cleaned their rifles and guns and honed knives and tomahawks while telling stories about other rescue attempts; warning those less experienced about dangers they may not be familiar with. Some swore strange things about what they were going to do to the war party when they caught them. Their women were baking biscuits and packing jerky for the men to take. There was no joking or laughing, each of these people had been involved in situations like this in the past. The Indians were good at fighting. Many of these men might not return at all.

John and Tom had followed the trail of the war party until nearly dark to determine if Rachel was still alive. They would chase the Indians anyway, but they wanted to be sure she had not been killed along the trail, as often happened to prisoners who couldn't keep up. John and Tom had stopped at the bottom of a small hill. It looked as though the Indians were heading toward Sweet Root; north and east of the fort. The Indians had doubled back to confuse pursuers. They would probably turn and cross the mountains far to the north of Fort Cumberland.

With this information, they returned to the fort to see if Michael and Nemesis had recruited the needed men. By knowing where to pick up the trail at first light, they felt they could come up with the war party before dark the next day and get in close during the night. This would be a race of endurance. Once the Indians crossed the Ohio River, they would be out of reach. Not many woodsmen would agree to go so deep into that unfamiliar and unforgiving territory. They had to catch them before they lost themselves in that wilderness.

John used a method that was as old as time to insure that the men were awake before morning: He simply took a long drink of water just before going to bed. The need to relieve himself would wake him well before daylight. But he didn't need the water. He couldn't sleep. Long before daylight he had everyone up and moving into the damp Appalachian morning. The pre-dawn glow made just enough light for the rescue party to cross Wills Creek and head east and north through a maze of hollows and narrow bottoms. They would go to the last track they saw yesterday and pick up the trail.

This war party knew what they were doing by staying east of Fort Cumberland. Had they crossed Wills Creek and headed west on Nemacolin's Trail, they could have been tracked and run down in the steep mountains, but they had traveled north and east between Evittes and Tussy Mountain, where they could ambush anyone following. Anyone following would be slowed by a need to move cautiously. Moving into the familiar territory surrounding the great warrior path let them put distance between themselves and a pursuing party.

It would be another half hour before the sun would cast its rays over the crest of Tussey Mountain when the rescue party reached the point that John and Tom had marked the evening before. The trail of the war party was easily located and Tom advised that men should be sent out on either side of the rescue party to move a little in advance and act as scouts. This meant slower travel. The dog fight in Johns soul was now a bloody war between impatience and caution.

·   ·   ·

Less than two miles to the north of where John and the rescue party were moving through the morning light Kitcheogeemaw woke Rachel and handed her jerked meat. This time she took it. She had reasoned in her mind that she may do without, but the baby inside her needed food. She looked around at the resting place; the others were quickly preparing to break camp. Kitcheogeemaw untied her hands and loosened the prisoner tie that was around her neck. He was very concerned about Rachel; more than any prisoner he ever had in his power. She did not know it, but she would be his sister. He would do all he could to keep her safe, but he would do even more to keep her prisoner... but he would still let her die before he let her be taken. When she was made his sister by ritual, he would die to protect her, but ritual was far away.

He led her to one side of the clearing where she made her toilet behind a

43

tree while he held to the end of the prisoner tie. She finished and he handed her the long ties that formed the leash. The designs on the neck band were powerful and the tie must stay on, but she could be free enough to move quickly; the party needed to move very quickly. Kitcheogeemaw handed her a pair of moccasins to put on and took her shoes. He threw the shoes into the thicket.

The wounded warrior was mounted on her horse now, and she had to walk. The party walked up the game trail through the increasing light. They had traveled only a short distance when a bird call was heard. Kitcheogeemaw signaled his men to stop, then answered with a responding call. More painted warriors started to emerge from the forest. They seemed to come up through the ferns and laurel like a fog.

Twelve warriors silently appeared. Greetings were exchanged. The new party's leader and Kitcheogeemaw were well known to each other. The two leaders stood a little off from the rest of the warriors, and looked at Rachel without actually showing the full curiosity each had for her. Rachel watched the two leaders talk. Kitcheogeemaw looked up as Yellow-Hand walked over and joined the conversation. Yellow-Hand pointed toward Rachel. Kitcheogeemaw and Rachel's eyes met. Kitcheogeemaw looked away as though embarrassed and Yellow Hand continued his conversation pointing down the trail in the direction from which they had come the night before.

As she watched she realized they were planning an ambush of the rescue party. Rachel felt the blood drain from her face. John! Terrible thoughts were building empires in her mind. Seeing her face pale and guessing she understood the meaning of their talk, Kitcheogeemaw had her taken away. Two warriors were assigned to lead her away, the one following kept the ends of the leash in his hands. If she did not obey, one jerk would choke her and pull her from her feet. She thought it sad that men knew so much about putting halters on other people. Her fetters made her think of Nem.

．　．　．

Kitcheogeemaw's eyes followed the departing people. A warrior led the seriously wounded warrior on the horse and two other injured warriors walked behind. Two older warriors that were escorting Rachel followed them. Kitcheogeemaw could barely hide his concern. They were over 20 nights from the village. Until the ritual his first responsibility was to his

44

warriors; and the woodsmen that would follow were dangerous men.

Kitcheogeemaw watched Pipe, the leader of the other party, strip down, paint up and get ready for war along with Yellow-Hand. Pipe had been convinced to attack any woodsmen that followed. They would be here soon if they were coming, but if they did not come, so much the better.

A warrior from Pipe's war party led a pack horse. He looked at his friends before he turned and led it in the direction Rachel and the other warriors had gone. In a moment Kitcheogeemaw followed.

Pipe sent out two warriors with instructions to locate any one approaching, count them, see how well they were armed, and return with the information. Yellow-Hand had advised Pipe of an ideal location to set up the intended ambush; Pipe instructed the two warriors to meet them at that place. Within minutes after the two scouts left, the war party was moving back down the trail toward a violent meeting with John Phares and his friends.

CHAPTER TEN

The morning sun was streaming down through the trees. The hollow sounds of a woodpecker drumming on the trunk of a dead tree could be heard on the side of the hill above the rushing waters that cooled the depths of Sweet Root gap. John was intently studying the ground for scuff marks, displaced stones, or anything that would indicate recent human activity. They had lost the trail when the Indians split up over rocky ground. Other men were spread out on both sides of the creek and up the sides of the ridges looking for signs of the war party. It would be easy to find Indian trails, but John wanted to find Rachel.

Nemesis rode up to John and said, "She didn't go that way!" He could see that John hadn't found anything certain yet. Hoof beats were heard and Tom and Michael rode up. John and Nemesis turned toward them as they approached. Tom leaned forward on his horse and said, "They didn't split north either!" John answered quietly. "They're going west!"

A big man rode up to the men. He was called "King" because he was as arrogant as the aristocracy across the ocean, but the man thought people called him that because of his ability to lead. He usually spent his time in taverns telling about great exploits that no one else could remember. But he was willing to fight and he could shoot better than anyone else in the country. King looked down at John from his stud horse and said, "I could have told you they were going west. I knew it all the time! Let's go kill some injuns! You guys are wasting my time!"

Tom always disliked being around King. He didn't hide his disdain very well. If men had not been so badly needed, he would have made sure that King was not included in this rescue attempt. Tom said, "King, John's got more at stake than you do. Let him call the shots!"

John advised the gathering men that Sweet Root Gap was about a half mile from where they were and it looked like the Indians were going to cut through the gap, go up to the Loyalhanna and out that way. Let's get to the gap then we'll see how things stand."

The men traveled quickly without flankers. Massive timber that had fallen began to block the way. Thick moss covered the rocks that began to jut up from the ground. The horses slipped and skidded across the rocks, stirring mosquitoes. As the group of rescuers approached the entrance to Sweet Root Gap John was in the lead, his eyes searching to the right and left for any sign left by the Indians. He hoped especially to see the tracks of a small foot that could only be made by Rachel. John suddenly stopped his horse and signaled for everyone else to stop. "This must be their camp site," he said.

"It looks like they had more than one wounded person with them. I make it at least two" said John, pointing to the ground.

Tom said, "I knew Josh wouldn't go down easy!"

Michael was out of his saddle and into the thicket where he picked up two small shoes and said, "John, I think she's alright. Look here!" John took the shoes from him and held them gently for a moment then placed them in the folds of his hunting shirt. He thought he could still feel her warmth in the leather soles. This indeed was proof that Rachel was alive and that they intended to keep her alive. John felt that they had given her moccasins so she could travel and keep up. As long as she was alive, there was hope.

"Alright," said John, "mount and go slowly. We don't want to back them into a corner. We want to surprise them. They'll kill Rachel if they think they can't escape."

A squirrel scolded them as they entered Sweet Root Gap. Tom pulled his horse to a stop and said, "Feels bad here...."

King rode up and said, "What's wrong?"

John said, "From here on we take it real easy. Tom's right; I've got the same feeling he has."

They looked up into the darkness of the gap. The noise of the cold stream almost drowned out the sounds of the grouse high on the mountain.

A man whispered, "If we keep the pressure up they won't have time to set up an ambush." King agreed, saying, "You're going to let them get away!"

King rode up to the front of the group looked back over his shoulder and said, "You all are worse than women; they're going to get away. They wouldn't be stupid enough to stay in this country this long. Let's get through so we can catch them. COME ON, let's get 'em!" He slapped his horse on the rump and it scampered into the mouth of the gap. Several of the men hesitated, then followed, leaving Tom, John, Nemesis and Michael behind.

John said, "If that idiot gets her killed, I'll take his scalp myself."

The four men kicked up their horses to catch up with King and the others. It was still possible they could talk some sense into them before they ran into trouble.

King George failed to notice the broken spider webs that drifted in the air far away from the path. He failed to notice that there were no animals moving and that mosquitoes had been disturbed among the rocks on either side. He failed to notice the men who followed were slowing down as they began to feel uneasy. He failed to notice the Indian who ran a spear through him. As he rode between a thick laurel bush and a giant hemlock tree that bordered the path the spear went through him from back to front. It was a small spear with an iron tip, but it was big enough to stop the best shot in the country from firing his gun ever again. At the same time King saw the spear head that paralyzed his breathing, shots were heard. War whoops rang out. The second man was hit with an arrow and two bullets at the same time. He was dead before he fell from his horse. The man behind him attempted to turn his horse and flee, but was too deep into the ambush. He was knocked out of his saddle by two warriors, one with a tomahawk, the other one with a war club. Both used their weapons on the rescuer's head and body. The fourth rescuer managed to get his horse turned and even managed to scream, "INDIANS!"

Tom, the hard core veteran, looked into the clouds of black powder smoke as he dodged an arrow. He glanced at Nem and said, "Wonder what ever made him notice there was Indians about?" He and Nemesis were dismounting. Horses were a hindrance in this narrow place.

Gun shots and arrows took their toll on the young man who still yelled to warn them. His yells became less sharp. Then he was quiet. Only his horse came past Tom and Nem.

Only war cries could be heard now. They were close. Their sounds echoed through the gap. Tom and Nemesis shot, each wounding his target. They started to reload. Michael rode up, but before he could dismount, his horse went down. He managed to get out of the saddle. Some of the shots that hit his horse had passed through his leg. Michael struggled to get to his feet and turn his gun on the warriors that seemed to be growing from the stones around them. Two warriors faced him; one just reloading his gun and the other closing with a tomahawk. John rode into the middle of it all. He shot the one and Michael swung his gun toward the Indian who had just

48

finished loading his gun. Both Michel and the warrior, only a few feet away from each other, pulled their triggers at the same time. Both had large caliber smooth bore guns and both were hit with the full force of each other's gunshot.

Michael was slammed back by the power of the heavy ball and fell under the thrashing feet of his wounded, screaming horse. The wounded animal trampled his lifeless body as it struggled to regain its feet, then ran wildly through the very middle of the ambush and over several of the combatants. The warrior Michael shot collided with the base of a huge tree, his lifeless body sagged into the sitting posture of a person unconcerned with the activity that was playing out in front of him.

Tom saw his son die and he could do nothing to stop it. He closed in, trying to get to his son, shooting one Indian close by, then dodging a war club. His left arm suddenly went numb as he was hit by a second war club. The club had shattered his upper arm, but Tom kept his feet and clubbed his attacker one-handed with his empty gun, causing red, green and black paint to mixed with the blood of the man it was supposed to protect. The Indian went down and stopped moving.

More Indians appeared from up and down the ambush site. Tom was cut off from Michael's body and unable to get to him. John's horse went down in the new barrage of shots. Nemesis' horse spooked and escaped back the way it had come. War whoops continued mingling with the screams of the wounded as the Indians moved in.

John and Nemesis tried to reach Tom. Nemesis shot one Indian as he fought his way to Tom. He punched another, driving him into the ground. It seemed nothing could stop him let alone slow him down. Tom and an Indian struggled together until Nemesis hit him with a fist that bent heavy iron all day long. John and Nemesis grabbed Tom and pulled him into the thickest brush they could find and crouched down as Yellow-Hand and two warriors cautiously approached. There were still enough war cries to cover their sounds as they moved farther and farther into the rocks and thickets.

. . .

The fighting was over and moments later war whoops were now heard only when a wounded woodsman was dispatched with the tomahawk, or enslaved

49

forever by a scalping knife. Yellow-Hand walked over to the final wounded white man who was too wounded to move and scalped him. This was a great raid for Yellow-hand. As the eyes of his prisoner glazed over in death, another warrior pried a double flint gun from his fingers. He picked up the gun, looked at it, shot off both barrels into the air with a war whoop, then waved the rare trophy above his head. It was the first double barrel gun he had ever seen.

Yellow-Hand's eyes narrowed and he reached for the gun. Words were exchanged that made it plain to anyone listening or watching that Yellow-Hand had as much as he would get without a fight: He had the scalp only because he was the first man to reach the disabled man. The warrior's hand went to the tomahawk stuck in his belt. Yellow-Hand took a step back then turned and walked away with only the bloody scalp of the dead rescuer as his trophy.

John, Tom and Nemesis found a good hiding place and ceased moving, not even taking full breaths least some sound or motion betray them to these Indians. The Indians didn't wait long. They were ready to get away. They lost too many warriors and knew their power was not strong in this place. As the warriors crossed the gap John whispered, "Come on, let's move."

The men crawled deeper into the thicket and away from the battleground.

Several miles later Tom's arm was swollen and making him light-headed from the pain. John called a halt and asked Nemesis to see if he could do anything for Tom's arm, while he went back down the trail to keep watch.

Nemesis worked on the arm. Tom seemed to feel no pain. As quiet as breath he whispered, "Michael. I seen him die… We'll come back when we can care for him proper." Nemesis nodded, tied the last binding strap on Toms arm and said, "… But he got the one that got him."

In a few minutes Nemesis had Tom's arm supported with a piece of shirt and tied it to Tom's chest so his arm couldn't move or bleed again. When John returned he brought a hat filled with water. Desperately thirsty, Tom drank and passed he remainder to Nem.

John said, "It don't look like they care to follow us… How's your arm?"

"I can manage," said Tom

John looked at Nemesis and said, "I'm going on. . . I know they will go straight to the Ohio River. You take Tom back with you.... It's coming on night." Tom words were quiet but forceful. "You tell yourself what to do, I'll tell me what to do . . . I'm coming with you." John wondered how anyone could love a world that did not hold friends . . .brothers. . .as true as this. John just nodded, nothing more need be said.

Nem pulled Tom to his feet and in a moment John moved into the gap again.

CHAPTER ELEVEN

Rachel was sitting under a tree in a state of exhaustion, barely aware of the activity going on around her. The broad murky river gurgled past. It was rather quiet in spite of the obvious power and weight of the water. The war party had arrived just before dark the evening before, and worked most of the night building a canoe. They chose a tall elm that was almost 30 feet to the first branch. Four warriors worked to carefully peel the bark away in one sheet without piercing it. Once it was down they clamped the ends shut and bent them up, braced the sides open and lashed long poles alongside to help it keep its shape. The big piece of bark looked like a sloppy boat, but it was a boat that could cross the Ohio River.

The tree they had peeled to make the canoe was so bright and pale that it looked like someone had whitewashed it with lime and water. It was on the very bank of the river and could be seen for a great distance. It made a perfect place to leave another memorial. This one was a celebration memorial. Every warrior moving up or down the River could read the news about how great this war party was. Rachel watched as a warrior painted figures on the tree with a mixture of charcoal and grease. A daub of vermilion drew attention to the important record. The figures would tell anyone who knew how to read who these warriors were, that they had taken many scalps and had captured a prisoner. Rachel's eyes were drawn to the stick figure that represented her — a red X with a dot at the top representing her head and little marks that represented feet at the bottom. Other marks represented scalps the warriors had taken, one of which was Joshua's. A canoe was drawn. It held figures representing each warrior, and above each warrior were symbols of his clan.

Kitcheogeemaw was checking on the wounded warriors. The night's rest had improved their strength, and once they were on the other side of the river, the war party would be able to slow down and give them a chance to gain needed rest. Rest would also help Rachel as much as the wounded warriors. She had never been so worn out in her life; her feet were sore, but in better shape than they would have been had she not been accustomed to going bare footed. Her head still ached, but less severely now.

A shadow fell over Rachel. Kitcheogeemaw had approached and was motioning for her to follow him to the finished canoe. The warriors were quickly loading it with the bundles and other possessions captured during their raids. Rachel was placed loaded in the center with the warrior Joshua wounded. In a moment they shoved off. Warriors were hanging on the sides of the canoe or gripping the tails of the horses, off to either side. To the young warriors the dangerous crossing was fun. They laughed, paddled, and splashed the horses toward the direction they wanted them to swim.

As the canoe moved downriver with the current and away from the wall of trees that bordered the water, she looked back at the shore line and the painted tree. The tree suddenly seemed lonely. Warriors no longer buzzed around like guardian bees and it looked abandoned. Then she noticed the growing field of water that increased the distance between her and the tree. Never in her life had she seen a river this big. She could walk across the Potomac in some places, but she knew with each paddle stroke this river could never be crossed by wading. The summer air could not stop an icy coldness from gripping her throat as the massive river seemed to laugh because she could not swim. She could not swim.

Even in the morning sunshine that makes everything seem better, the river seemed want to pull her body down, to wrap it's coldness around her as it effortlessly became a barrier between herself and John. For the first time in two days she spoke aloud. A feeling of hopelessness tightened her words to a whisper. "Dear Jesus, please help me." Then between sobs she confided her fear in prayer, "I can't swim…How can I get back to John?"

As she prayed she lowered her eyes to the wet bark that formed the canoe, but voices of the Indians became louder than the water: something was drawing their attention to the river bank they had just left. As she turned to look with them her head was pulled back violently by the wounded warrior sitting behind her. He had grabbed a handful of her hair and raised a tomahawk over her head. Rachel didn't care if her hair was torn loose; she must look back to see what had caused so much excitement. As hair tore from its roots she was able to see two figures standing next to the painted tree. One was a giant black man, Nemesis; the other was John! As she watched, a third figure, Tom Thomas, was coming out of the trees into the light.

She saw John raise his rifle.

Kitcheogeemaw had stopped paddling and turned to look at John and yelled in Wyandot, "Go home! Do not follow or she dies!" Another warrior repeated the warning in English. The warrior holding Rachel's hair raised his tomahawk and shook Rachel's head as though he were moving it into a better position to tomahawk her.

John's legs began to wobble when he saw the tomahawk held above Rachel's head. He quickly moved to brace his gun against a small oak sapling, dropping the heavy barrel to rest on a fork about shoulder high. John took a breath, and a second sight. His finger tightened on the trigger. He had shot deer at distances greater than this. Sweat broke out on his forehead. He wanted so much to shoot. She was so close and he was so powerless except for this rifle. There was nothing left but the round ball of lead that lay nestled against the charge of black powder. The painted men were taking his life, his dreams. They were stealing his wife and unborn child from him. He tried to gauge the wind but there were no leaves to betray its speed or course. He tried to gauge the distance but they were moving with the water. He wished for shadows to stop the metal gun barrel from glaring and making ripples in the air between his sights. He tried to make his heart stop beating so it wouldn't shake the gun. He held fast and still without blinking. His finger slowly increased the pressure against the trigger. His front sight rested squarely on Kitheogeemaw. He thought again and moved the front sight so that he could kill one who held the tomahawk above her head. But...the bullet could go through him and hit Rachel.

There were two dogs fighting for Johns mind now; one was hope and the other was hopelessness. John knew that hopelessness was fighting to make him shoot. Hope was telling him she would stay alive until he could find some way to get her back. Tears began to blur his vision. Hopelessness was winning the dogfight. As the tears began to spill down John's expressionless face Nemesis softly laid a hand on his shoulder, saying, "John, don't shoot. The others will kill her...."

The moment for John's shot had passed, but he still held the front sight on one of them, then another. As they became obscured by the flickering light reflected from the moving water he lowered his rifle and walked toward the water. He followed the bank down river. The Indians were almost across now. Walking with the water he was oblivious to the brush and branches that seemed to spread their bony fingers to block his way. A hundred yards from the peeled tree, he stepped to the edge of the bank, breathed in deeply and screamed out simple words. He used his strength and abused his voice as if he never needed to use it again: "I LOVE YOU RACHEL... I LOVE YOU... I LOVE YOU, RACHEL... On and on he screamed until he knew she could no longer hear him. His rifle was forgotten, useless, in his hand. His head collapsed upon his chest as the murky water slipped past and he finally he could only whisper... I love you... I love you... I'm sorry."

The leading Indians were reaching the far shore, just out of rifle range. Unconfined by the water, they scrambled to the canoe for guns the moment it reached shallow water. Kitcheogeemaw sent the wounded warrior take Rachel into the woods out of danger and out of sight, and he turned to face John. The warriors began to shoot across the broad river. They wouldn't think of swimming back to attack for they knew they would be killed by those marksmen before they could reach them... but they could shoot. They might even draw blood. Trade guns and captured guns were loaded, fired and reloaded.

Shots splashed in the water in front of John and whacked into the trees behind him. He stood still. As the Indians continued shooting Nemesis yelled for John to get back to the tree line. John was beyond hearing or caring what happened to him, so as the bullets splashed around them, Nemesis ran to John and pulled him into the trees away from the river; away from the guns, ...and away from Rachel.

CHAPTER TWELVE

The woodsmen knew what happened to prisoners if they couldn't keep up. Rachel could be killed for being unable to keep up the pace. Even if she survived the journey and finally reached the distant village, she could be burned alive by the tribe as repayment of some wrong they felt. Sometimes any Indian who desired to do so could hurt her. John's last glimpse of her would haunt his dreams for months to come. She looked so small and defenseless next to the warrior holding onto her hair, dragging her into the forest.

Safely hidden by the trees, Nemesis released his hold letting John regain his footing, but grabbed John's arm and continued tugging. "You gonna walk now? You gonna get us killed!" As they reached the cover of the tree line, the shooting stopped and the Indians disappeared into the trees on the west shore of the river.

Nemesis knew what it was to have your family taken from you and not be able to do anything about it. His own memories of were fresh in his mind as he said, "I know how you feel, John, my wife was taken from me....by civilized men . . . but you can't do anything for them if you're dead. Now, I'm going to buy my woman from those civilized men...You can buy yours back from them heathens!" John looked up into Nem's solemn black eyes and saw deeper into the soul of the man than he ever could before. Rachel being taken had opened a door between the two men that John hadn't even known existed. John was speechless. He was like Nemesis. And Nemesis was like him. He was not alone in this paralyzing sadness. It wasn't that Nem's pain made his easier. It didn't. But John knew without doubt he was not alone, and this one man's strength somehow became his own. In that moment he loved this great man that no one else could fully see. Together they walked up stream to the peeled tree.

The three woodsmen checked the priming on their flintlock rifles, and arranged their gear for the long walk back to the Ohio Company trading post on Wills Creek. They thought they might be between the war party that had taken Rachel and the war party they had fought two days earlier, so they decided to head south for half a day before turning east, avoiding trouble if possible. Nemesis and Tom moved out. As he passed the painted tree John looked at the figure representing Rachel, then reached up to touch it. The greasy charcoal smeared onto his fingers. He gave the west shoreline a last lingering look. The abandoned canoe was seen drifting near the river's edge so far away they could never reach it. He turned to follow Tom and Nemesis into the humid air of the shadowed forest.

· · ·

As the sun set, water lapped against the canoe that had drifted ashore. In the shade of the west bank there was only one lone warrior that Kitcheogeemaw had left behind to make certain they were not followed. He remained hidden in the screen of leaves beyond the lapping water, watching and waiting. He would stay there until just after first light, then he would catch up with his people.

· · ·

Several miles to the east, Pipe signaled for his warriors to stop. They had seen no danger since the day before. They did not want to reach the river during the hours of darkness. They needed a chance to scout the area before they exposed themselves crossing the river. In a short while they had a fire burning that couldn't be seen more than a few feet away. Several pieces of meat were placed on sticks and roasted. The last rays of the setting sun reflected off the clouds, casting an eerie pink glow upon the painted men. In the last few moments of daylight, the warriors recounted, in low voices, the activities of the past few days.

CHAPTER THIRTEEN

Rachel awakened suddenly; she was trembling and shaking because the sound of a gunshot had mixed with the dream she was having. The dampness of the early morning and the aching in her body brought back the nightmare of being awake. She was no longer tied up every night, and had freedom of movement within sight of Kitcheogeemaw wherever they camped. Rachel had even started tending the warrior who was most severely wounded. She wouldn't touch him because she didn't want to, and she wasn't sure she would be allowed to, but she brought water and wood for cooking and comfort. The other two wounded warriors were healing well and did not need any more doctoring.

The warrior who had fired the shot she heard returned to camp with a huge turkey he had killed. It was the first fresh meat they had obtained in the deep forest of the Ohio country. Hunting was always better along streams or around lakes, but one could starve a little when traveling. The Indians felt safe now. The warriors knew that they were now in good hunting grounds. Fresh growth of young saplings and bushes were a welcome sight. The huge charred trunks of the mighty monarchs of the virgin forest contrasted with the fresh green of the younger forest growth. The new growth provided fresh crops for wildlife, and the wildlife fed the warriors.

A flutter of wings drew Rachel's attention to the creek next to their camp. The early morning sunlight flashed on the wings of a crane as it caught a fish from a pool of water formed by a bend in the creek. The excitement of the warriors was very evident. Rachel was aware that something good had just happened but did not realize that the crane was a great power to some of the Wyandot people.

The turkey was cut up, put on several sticks and propped over the fire. The spirits of the warriors seemed to improve, much talk and laughter was going around the campfire as the men devoured the half cooked piece of meat. Kitcheogeemaw handed Rachel a handful of meat that he had torn from his own share. Without hesitation she ate the meat and licked the juices from her fingers. Kitcheogeemaw and the warriors decided to camp a day longer to hunt. It would give them a chance to rest, get food, make moccasins, and perhaps give Pipe a chance to catch up with them. After all, the crane getting food right in front of them was a good omen.

A temporary shelter was being built. They chopped down several saplings and tied another between two trees. Next they laid the other saplings inches apart, with the butt ends pushed into the ground and the small ends resting on the parallel sapling. Rachel helped gather pine branches and spread them on the ground inside the shelter. Bark was peeled from a large tree and overlapped on the slanted saplings. The white pine branches would keep the occupants off of the damp ground and give them a comfortable, sweet smelling bed.

Another warrior built a frame of wood that he split from a sapling and set it near the fire in preparation for the expected venison that would be brought in this day. The warriors who were not recovering from wounds had left to hunt or check their back trail.

By the time the temporary camp had been completed, two deer had been brought in. Rachel was in the middle of the activity, skinning, roasting and then cutting the rest into thin strips, and spreading the meat on the drying rack to make jerky for the rest of the trip to the village.

They needed moccasins so a warrior split the skulls of the deer and cooked the brain in the skull cap very slowly. With a stick he removed unwanted parts to make a kind of a thick mixture that resembled pudding. Another warrior had stretched the deer hides by driving wooden stakes in the ground and had started scraping fat and membrane from the hide. After the brain had been cooked to the consistency that the warrior preferred, he started to rub one brain into a hide while another warrior started rubbing the other brain into the other deer hide. It took several hours to dry the hides by stretching them near the fire until no moisture remained. The warriors were wet with sweat but by night fall the hides were tanned soft and supple. Then the hides were smoked over the fire so they would remain soft whether they were wet or dry. A low smoky fire would be kept under the hides until the color of the smoke showed through the opposite side of the hide.

Rachel went to the creek and started gathering the new growth of cat tail plants that were just showing above the surface of the water. This would be a welcome addition to the meal because of their fresh sweet taste this time of year.

Kitcheogeemaw was sitting on the bank of the creek smoking and watching her as she gathered the cat tails. She reminded him of his sister, Catches-the-Wind, who never gave up. He noticed that Rachel had the same habit Catches-the-Wind had: She tossed her head to keep the hair out of her face when it wasn't tied back. Like Catches-the-Wind, when she saw a job that needed to be done, she would do it.

Kitcheogeemaw's thoughts were interrupted by movement beyond the creek at the far boundary of line of sight. He knew that all of his party were in camp. He motioned for Rachel to go back with the others. Two warriors grabbed their guns and rolled out of sight into the brush then slipped down the creek toward the movement. The rest stayed where they were, not moving. There was no panic. Pipe and his party were expected, but it was still a point of honor not to be taken by surprise by friend or foe: An enemy might kill them, but it was certain that friends would not let them forget the joke.

Peering into the forest Rachel could see nothing unusual, but sounds reached her that she would never forget. They made her blood run cold. The scalp yell. It was repeated six times. An "aw", then raising to the "oh" sound in a long drawn out yell that lasted as long as the warrior giving it had breath. There was one yell for each head taken. She counted six yells from the approaching group of warriors. A deep fear and coldness enveloped her. Was John's scalp the reason for one of these yells? The sounds were dreadful to hear and well calculated to strike terror in a person hearing one for the first time, especially when it could mean a loved one was dead.

As Pipe's war party approached camp, the warriors were firing their guns and finishing the death whoops. The warriors in camp fired their guns off in return and gave death whoops suitable to the number of scalps they had taken. Kitcheogeemaw fired his gun and gave the death whoop that represented Rachel's captivity

. . .

Rachel couldn't take her eyes from Yellow-Hand as he entered camp. He had two scalps tied to a stick that had been stretched on willow hoops. Red paint was smeared on the skin side of each scalp and the hair had been carefully combed to present the best appearance possible for such prized trophies.

Rachel recognized Joshua's hair. She was thankful that she didn't know who the other belonged to. She looked for John's scalp among the scalps being displayed.

The last words she heard John yell as she was dragged away from the river were, "I love you, Rachel." If she had a last memory of John she would rather it be those words instead of a vision of his scalp. Then she remembered she had something else that would make her remember John. Her hands gently stroked her stomach and she felt a little stronger.

The warriors greeted each other. They were brothers, cousins and friends who had survived war and shared a bond that only people who have been involved in fighting for one another can understand.

Yellow-Hand walked up to Rachel and threw the two scalps in her lap and laughed as he said in broken English, "One of these your man!"

Rachel seeing the familiar hair in her lap whispered Joshua's name. Then she recognized Michael's scalp. She started to weep. Yellow-Hand grabbed the scalps off her lap and fastened them to his belt. Rachel watched him with a look of utter contempt on her face.

It was a dangerous night for Rachel. Three warriors had been killed by the white men and some of the recently arrived warriors wanted her as payment. One of Pipe's warriors grabbed Rachel and attempted to paint her face black with some charcoal from the fire as a sign of a condemned prisoner. They wanted to see red blood run on white flesh, and hear the screams from their victim that would appease the spirits of their dead companions.

Kitcheogeemaw made it plain that this would be decided by the council of the elders when they arrived at the village. They had many nights of travel ahead of them and a decision such as this, which could cause war between brothers, was too important to enter into on the trail. The look on Kitcheogeemaw's face, and the knowledge that they were facing imminent death if they crossed this man, satisfied Pipe's war party. They recognized the right of conquest. Rachel was under Kitcheogeemaw's power.

The subject was not closed however; there would be many arguments for Rachel's death by torture and fire. These men had lost relatives and the matter would not be forgotten. Kitcheogeemaw took the prisoner tie from his pack and wrapped it around Rachel's neck then tied it. The designs woven into the belt made it plain to any Indian that this was Kitcheogeemaw's property and she was under his power. He then gently pushed Rachel into the shelter. Aware that a debate raged about her, she sat next to his pack and stayed out of sight as much as possible. From this night on she knew that Kitcheogeemaw was the only place of safety.

The following afternoon they approached a Shawnee town located on the west shore of the Sciota River. They stopped long enough for the warriors to paint their faces. Kitcheogeemaw painted Rachel's cheeks and forehead with red paint. The scalps were suspended from a pole several feet long and this was used as a trophy banner which preceded the war party. They walked to the bank of the river where they could see the Shawnees on the other side.

Pipe gave a loud, "Hallo" to get the attention of several Indians, who could be seen performing some type of ceremony. They were roasting objects hanging from a long pole suspended between two trees. It appeared to be the end of the ceremony and people were wandering off into the village, leaving several children and two or three adults poking at the objects suspended from the pole. The fire that had been burning under the pole was now a dying bed of coals.

Pipe's warriors fired off their guns as a sign of friendship and greeting, but more importantly, the loud noise would frighten away bad spirits that might follow them from the white man's country. Scalp yells broke through the air and several occupants of the village fired their guns in return. The Shawnee Indians spotted Rachel with the Wyandots, and the yelling became more intense because they expected another celebration. They launched canoes and dugouts and paddled toward the Wyandots.

Rachel was placed in a canoe with Kitcheogeemaw behind her. The straps of the prisoner tie were held tightly in his hand. As they approached the shore, a sight so shocking she nearly retched greeted Rachel. She could never forget its horror. The objects of the earlier celebration still hung suspended from the pole. But now she recognized what they were: The things that seemed so unimportant from a distance were fire blackened heads, arms and legs of white prisoners that had been roasted just prior to the approach of Kitcheogeemaw's war party.

Two lines of people were being formed as she approached the village. Each line faced the other about eight feet apart and extended into the town. Participants were waving switches and sticks. Kitcheogeemaw motioned for Rachel to stay in the canoe, but he got out and approached a group of middle aged men who appeared to be the leaders in the village. After several minutes of conversation and shaking of heads and motioning of hands, two women came to the canoe and pulled Rachel onto the beach and in broken English told her to follow them.

The two lines of people started breaking up when they saw they were not going to have a victim to run their gauntlet, but several women and children shook their sticks and grabbed at Rachel. Some of them pulled her hair as she was led toward a house that was about 20 feet long and 14 feet wide. It was larger than her and John's cabin. The sides and roof were made of small poles and covered with bark. An old blanket hung across the opening at one end making a kind of door. An old woman standing near the opening said some words. When Rachel failed to understand or respond, she hit Rachel with a piece of firewood, knocking her to the ground. Two of the women screamed something at the old crone and she retreated, still voicing unknown complaints and threats. Rachel's jaw was already beginning to swell under a fresh a cut that was bleeding.

The women pushed Rachel into the long house and left her alone. In the center of the house was a fire and above it hung a boiling kettle holding venison and Indian corn. Rachel sat by the small fire and attempted to stop her jaw from the bleeding. In a few minutes the two women returned.

One woman looked at her wound and said something in Shawnee to her companion and both laughed. The other woman dipped some meat and corn out of the kettle, put it in a wooden bowl and handed it to Rachel. She had not eaten since that morning and after walking all day, was ready for any meal. The other woman handed Rachel a lump of maple sugar in lieu of salt.

Sounds of loud yelling and singing were heard coming from the other side of the small village. The Shawnee and Wyandot warriors were drinking whiskey and bragging on their recent exploits and capture of prisoners.

Kitcheogeemaw did not want Rachel in danger. He paid a fine knife and some of the booty he had captured to have two women look after her for the night. If he did not provide protection for Rachel, several of the warriors present, including Yellow-Hand, would take revenge on her.

Rachel's eyes grew heavy soon after she ate. As she started to lie down, one of the women pulled out a bear skin, several deer hides and an old blanket from a pile and handed them to Rachel. The woman pointed to a spot on the floor on the other side of the fire near the wall, indicating where she should sleep. Rachel was so tired that within seconds the bites from the fleas that occupied the blanket and hides were no longer noticed, and she was asleep. Her last thoughts were that when she slept outside the mosquitoes ate her up; inside, the fleas ate what is left.

Rachel was suddenly awakened by the firing of guns. Indians were yelling and banging against the sides of the long house and banging things against the roof of the building. She sat upright in terror. The two women patted her and in broken English one of them said, "Must drive away spirits of prisoners that were burned, much bad happen if not done."

In a few minutes she relaxed and sleep overcame her fears until she smelled meat cooking. She opened her eyes and saw one of the women cutting some venison into small pieces and putting them into hot bear's oil in a frying pan that was sitting on red coals in the fire pit. The woman picked up a pouch and sprinkled some dried herbs over the meat, then poured more bear's oil over the dish and let it fry. Next she put a small copper kettle of water on the fire to boil. Within minutes she put some tea into the water and set the pot aside to seep. Rachel then saw something she did not expect to see this far from civilization. The woman removed three cups and saucers of yellow ware from a pouch and set them out. The woman did not take the least notice of Rachel the whole time she was cooking.

When the food was done, she poured some tea in a cup and put some of the meat in a saucer and handed it to Rachel. Rachel had expected her to set the cup in the saucer, but when she thought about what the Indian woman did, seemed very reasonable to eat from the saucer and drink from the cup. The tea was the most welcome fare Rachel had tasted since she had been captured. It was green tea, sweetened with maple sugar. She was surprise that the tea seemed to ease the ache in her jaw. Rachel felt as though she would be able to face the day and its unknown events.

Soon after finishing this meal, a tapping beside the door was heard and when the blanket was thrown back Kitcheogeemaw entered. He had a frown and a wound on his face and appeared to be sick. He could see that Rachel's attention was drawn to the wound on his face and pointing to it he said, "Ah! Matowesa whiskey," indicating that he had gotten into a fight as a result of being influenced by the spirits of the whiskey. Kitcheogeemaw opened the bundle he had with him and produced several pieces of cloth and a pair of scissors which he gave to the women. Their husbands already had the knives he had promised. He thanked them and motioned for Rachel to pick up the bundle and follow him.

The activity of the village was just starting. Few people moving around. Kitcheogeemaw and Rachel did not draw any attention as they moved through the village and walked several hundred yards to where the rest of the war party was camped.

Kitcheogeemaw noticed the bruise and cut on Rachel's cheek when she leaned over to set the bundle down. A look of anger rose in his face as he asked in broken English, "They hurt you?" Rachel felt that he meant the two women who had looked after her. She shook her head no. He looked close at the wound, then he seemed to settle down.

The rest of the war party had just finished their breakfast, which consisted of a pot of boiled meat from the feast of the night before. The men brought out their pipes and started smoking, nothing would proceed until each man had a chance to finish his pipe.

Kitcheogeemaw lit his pipe that was taken from a bag that hung around his neck. The pipe bag made from the skin of a flying squirrel was well decorated with porcupine quills dyed in bright colors. He started to light the pipe but became very pale and put the pipe away. When the others finished their pipes, he turned to the men and said something in Wyandot to them. Those who were ready picked up their gear. The rest hurriedly finished getting themselves ready for the trail. They were all sore or sick due to the strong spirits they had drunk the night before. There were bruises and cuts on every man. One had an ear missing and had a bloody rag tied around his head. He was the last to fall in line as they staggered and walked toward the northwest and home.

Rachel knew to keep clear of these men as much as she possibly could. About mid-morning they were crossing a stream and Rachel slipped on a slime covered stone as she attempted to gain the shore. In falling she fell against the warrior following her and he nearly lost his balance. When she tried to stand, her head was suddenly pushed under the water. She was held there. She tried to scream but only got a mouthful of water. She could hear the man laughing as he let her get her head just out of the water enough to get a breath, and then plunged her head back under. She breathed in much water which caused her to choke. She thought she was going to die. Suddenly the hand that held her down was gone. Rachel came to the surface choking and gasping for breath. She crawled onto the bank of the stream before she realized that Kitcheogeemaw was standing knee deep in the water and in his sickness was as dangerous as she'd ever seen him. But his anger was not directed toward her. He was looking at Yellow-Hand who was sitting chest deep at his feet. The rest of the Indians were laughing at

Yellow-Hand, who was trying to get to his feet and rub a swollen spot on the side of his face at the same time.

Yellow-Hand's eyes met Rachel's and he looked at her with hate. There was no doubt in Rachel's mind that Yellow-Hand would like nothing better than to do her great harm. His fear of Kitcheogeemaw was the only thing keeping Rachel from terrible injury or death. Kitcheogeemaw turned without saying a word and walked down the trail, picking up his pack as he passed Rachel. He paid her no mind and Rachel was taken aback at his coldness toward her. She did not understand that the battle between Kitcheogeemaw and Yellow Hand had just become open and formal. Blows had been given and received. As Kitcheogeemaw walked on without looking back Rachel did not waste any time getting her bundle picked up so she could catch up to him. He might be cold to her, but others would like to kill her.

No stop was made until the sun was very low. By this time, Rachel was nearly crippled from spending most of the day walking in wet moccasins. The evening was turning colder and Rachel had wrapped her thin damp blanket around herself trying to get warm. She could not get near the fire because there was no room for her. In the darkness she felt a hand on her shoulder which made her jump. Kitcheogeemaw looked down at her and said, "Head pain gone, bad spirit of whiskey gone." Rachel understood that he had been suffering from a bad hangover all day, but it would be months before she understood the cost of Kitcheogeemaw's protection from Yellow Hand. Kitcheogeemaw motioned for her to move near the fire. As Rachel attempted to get up, the pain from walking in wet moccasins all afternoon made her wince and gasp.

Kitcheogeemaw told her to sit and he pulled the damp foot ware off her feet and saw their condition. He laid her moccasins near the fire and walked to the stream, searching the ground as though he were looking for something. In a short while he returned with a hand full of blue violets that had been pulled up by the roots. Kitcheogeemaw cut the roots away from the flowers and went to his pack and removed a piece of cloth. After tearing a small piece from the cloth, he wrapped the roots in it and made a poultice by mashing the roots with two stones. Kitcheogeemaw then divided the poultice by cutting the piece of cloth in half and wrapped them around Rachel's feet. In a while she started feeling better.

That night was full of wolves. Wolves had always frightened Rachel. The sound they made was so lonesome and haunting and whenever she heard them, no matter how much she fought it, her mind always went back to the evening ten years before, when she had lost her family to the scalping knife and tomahawk. After the Indians left wolves came to the smell of blood near the cabins. They ate all night long.

This night she was much disturbed by the howling of a great number of wolves that were only kept back by the fire and presence of the men. Rachel slept very little. Every time she dozed, she would wake up trembling from the reoccurring nightmare of that night and the fear of those wolves.

During the night her feet stopped hurting and became cold. She removed the poultice and retrieved her moccasins, which were within arm's reach and were now dry and warm from the fire. Kitcheogeemaw had placed her between the fire and himself. It was only toward morning that she was able to fall sound asleep.

At the first sounds of dawn, the rustling of leaves just outside the circle of warriors made Rachel sit bolt upright. She was expecting to see a wolf stalking her while the warriors were still sleeping. The ferocious animal that greeted her was only a gray squirrel that had just retrieved a treasure he had buried and was sitting up holding it between his paws. The squirrel appeared to be contemplating a small green root just starting to grow from the acorn it held. Rachel's sudden movement drew his attention to her and the squirrel bolted up the tree next to the sleeping warriors. A loud chorus of barking and screeching from the squirrel woke everyone.

The men seemed to take more than casual notice of the weather, and after a hurried conversation, two warriors left in the direction they had been heading the last several days. Within minutes the rest of the party followed. Later as they were approaching the crest of a hill, a gunshot was heard coming from the next ridge. In a short while, Rachel could see that the two warriors who had left ahead of them were busy cleaning a deer. She was very hungry. She had not eaten since the morning before and was as happy as the men upon seeing the fresh meat.

The day was getting darker as clouds blocked the rays of the sun. Kitcheogeemaw said something to the two hunters and after another short conversation, he led the men several hundred yards to a huge boulder that was protruding from the hillside, forming a two-sided type of shelter with an overhang. Kitcheogeemaw took several pinches of tobacco from his tobacco pouch and seemed to offer it to the area under the overhanging boulder. Then he held his hands to the sky and asked the spirits to let them enter this place of the ancient ones and to watch over them while they were there. Each of the warriors repeated the ceremony before entering the protected area.

Several of the men cut down some white pine saplings, trimmed the branches off and started a fire. Several dead saplings were dragged in for firewood. With everyone pitching in, a comfortable camp was made ready. The two warriors soon had the deer brought in, cut up and over the fire.

Rachel was busy spreading the pine branches under the over-hanging boulder as the rain started. It came down in sheets, but they all remained dry. Rachel could tell that this place had seen many campfires. Smoke stained the rocky shelter, and pieces of chipped flint, burnt bones, and broken pottery lay everywhere. Crude drawings were on the great boulder and some if the drawings represented animals never seen by them, their fathers, or grandfathers. They did not know any stories about these animals with heads that looked like a snake with big floppy looking ears and huge bodies and long hair; or animals with horns growing out of their nose; or cat-like creatures with long tusks-like front teeth. If these were real animals, they had lived before the memory of these men or anyone they knew. As darkness enveloped the camp site, the drawings seemed to come alive as the campfire's flickering light reflected off the ancient works of art.

The storm passed and it stopped raining before dawn. As daylight lit the interior of the ancient campsite, the men got ready to continue their journey. As they left the shelter, each man stopped to present a pinch of tobacco to the spirits of the ancient ones, before lighting their pipes. Each man presented his pipe to the spirits by holding the burning pipe to the sky and letting the smoke travel upward on the morning updraft created by warmth of the rising sun.

For the next several days the group passed through a changing landscape. Some nights they had plenty to eat and other times they had to go for as much as a day before any game was killed. Rachel moved with a tiredness she had never before experienced. Every morning became more difficult. The morning sickness that came with pregnancy would nearly overcome her at the start of each day's journey. Her clothes were worn to tatters and she was filthy and infested with fleas and lice. One afternoon, she happened to see her reflection in a stream where she was drinking. Her reflection in the water seemed to be an image of a woman much older than herself. The weakness she saw written in that face caused more concern than the pain caused by the Indian woman who had hit her with the piece of firewood.

Rachel felt she could not take another day of this punishment, but then she noticed a change in the demeanor of the men. They were in a country with many trees stripped of their bark and many bare trunks were painted with records of previous war expeditions. The war party was quiet and respectful as they made camp. Rachel was taken away from the war party to a place by herself, but she could still see the warriors clean and groom themselves, unroll their packs and dress in their finest clothes. Some chanted and some smoked. Two warriors approached a tree that showed their war party departing and painted figures showing their return with scalps and a prisoner. On the tree that Pipe's men had painted when they departed, they now drew the results of their expedition. The greasy charcoal showed three warriors dead and several scalps taken.

After grooming and painting himself, Kitcheogeemaw painted vermilion across Rachel's shoulders, tied his quelled prisoner strap more securely around her neck, and placed a rattle made with the toes of a deer in her hand. All this was to show that she was his possession. He sat in front of her and patiently taught her how he wanted the rattle to be shaken. At last he nodded his approval. Then he took the prisoner tie in his hand and motioned for her to follow the other warriors as he walked behind her. For the first time in a long time he had tied the band so tight that the unfinished quills threatened to break the skin of her neck in a hundred places: the decorated side of the band was beautiful, but the side against her neck was crude and painful.

Kitcheogeemaw led his war party away from Pipe's war party. When she looked over her shoulder, Rachel saw the men with Pipe painting their faces black. Their attitude was much different than Kitcheogeemaw's warriors.

CHAPTER FOURTEEN

As Rachel followed behind Kitcheogeemaw, she sensed excitement growing in the warriors. They rounded a bend in the path and began yelling, whooping and shooting off their guns. Within seconds, sounds of whooping and gunshots were heard. The sound increased and spread as the news of the returning war parties moved through the village. The scalp whoops were given, and as the Indians spotted Rachel, the yelling increased and the people started forming two lines leading from the edge of the village to the largest longhouse. Rachel's blood ran cold as she realized that this gauntlet was for her and couldn't be avoided this time. Her first thought went to the unborn child she carried. She faltered. Kitcheogeemaw touched her shoulder to get her attention and then motioned for her to continue to shake her rattle as they neared the village.

Rachel looked at Kitcheogeemaw. She had come to rely on him for her safety. He returned her look steadily, encouraging her with his eyes. Rachel had to fight to control the panic she felt. She had heard so many stories of what can happen to prisoners who couldn't complete the gauntlet. She knew that if she fell she would be at the mercy of these people, and she saw no friendly faces down this alley of screaming men, whooping women and children of all ages. Since it was a female who was about to run past them, each person was holding a switch or stick. Had it been a man, there would have been warriors present with more formidable weapons. She stepped forward shaking the rattle as instructed.

At last Kitcheogeemaw took the rattle from Rachel, untied and removed the prisoner strap, then ripped away the dress that was now nothing more than rags. Rachel tried to cover herself. Yellow-Hand jeered at her and said, "Welcome." The noise was tremendous. Rachel looked through the gauntlet. She was painfully aware of her nakedness. Then she remembered how even Jesus, the son of God, had been stripped of his clothing and she set her jaw and lifted her chin. Christ's dignity and determination had replaced her fear

70

and embarrassment. These people should be the ones embarrassed; she had done nothing to them. Rachel's dignity was made of more than clothing.

Yellow-Hand shoved Rachel hard and she took off running as fast as she could. Without the dress to hinder her steps she ran swiftly and with great power. Her sore feet were forgotten. The women showed no mercy as they tried to strike her when she passed between the lines. Rachel pushed her hand in one woman's face, knocking her down. She dodged the blows as best she could, but with every step she felt the burning of the switches and the numbing blows of the sticks. She tried to reach the safety of the longhouse at the end of the lines. If she fell and could not rise and make it to the longhouse, she would be deemed undesirable for adoption into their nation and could be beaten to death. She could not fall. She could not fail. She would carry her child to safety.

A 15-year-old boy stepped out with a large stick and she ran straight at him so he could not swing. The collision left the boy on the ground and a laugh erupted from those around him. The distraction enabled Rachel to gain a few free strides toward the council house. She continued to run and blows continued raining on her back.

Rachel was almost to the council house when a blow to the head stunned her. She barely maintained her balance long enough to stumble into the building.

When the blackness and confusion lifted she could sense the walls protecting her. In a short while an elderly woman and a young woman carrying a pot of hot water, entered the longhouse. Little Fawn cried when she saw the injuries the young white woman had suffered. In her heart, she had already adopted Rachel. This bleeding and bruised girl was not Rachel. Little Fawn knew nothing of a girl named Rachel. This girl was changed. Now this girl was her daughter, Catches-the-Wind. Little Fawn told the younger woman, Night-Bird-Singing, to set the water down and help her clean the wounds on Catches-the-Wind. She told the girl, "This is your sister now."

The two women tenderly cleaned Rachel and rubbed bear oil on her. They combed her hair and killed as many lice as they could. They rubbed bear oil into her hair and scalp and combed her hair again. When they had cleaned her as best they could, they wrapped her in a blanket.

Little Fawn called her son into the longhouse. Kitcheogeemaw entered. Little Fawn asked him to carry Catches-the-Wind to their lodge. He tenderly picked her up as if he were carrying a small child and carried her to his mother's lodge where he tenderly laid Rachel next to the small fire. He could openly express his admiration for this strong woman because now she was his sister. When he was satisfied that his mother had everything she needed for Rachel's comfort he told his mother that he must prepare for the council. "Warriors have died, and the whole war party captured Catches-The-Wind, and not me alone. I must present my case before the council; they will decide her fate. There is a call for blood from Yellow-Hand and from Pipe and his warriors. Strong words must be spoken and I must ask the Great Spirit for guidance in this matter."

There were tears in Little Fawn's eyes as she touched Kitcheogeemaw on the cheek and told him that the Great Spirit would not take away the daughter he had just given her.

Kitcheogeemaw left and went to prepare for the council. He did not remember to tell Little Fawn that Rachel was carrying a baby. The only thing on his mind was presenting a case to the elders that would secure Rachel for his mother. Had he captured Rachel by being the only one to lay hands on her, she would be his to do with as he pleased, but Yellow-Hand was part of the capture. And Pipe lost three men in the ambush of Rachel's potential rescuers.

In the quiet of the lodge Little Fawn turned Rachel on her stomach and pulled the blanket away from her back. She looked closely at the wounds and began to daub medicine on them. An old man sitting nearby mixed the medicines and handing them to her as he completed each batch. The old man was Little Fawn's brother, Jacob Laughing-Otter. As he mixed the medicine, he sang and chanted to give power to the medicine, and to entertain himself. Little Fawn also sang a soothing sad song as she doctored Rachel's back and head until Jacob interrupted his singing to bend down to see if Rachel was awake yet. She was not, so Jacob sat back up and continued singing and mixing more medicine. Jacob, leaning forward again, saw that Rachel's eyes were open.

Jacob sat back up, continued mixing a paste for her wounds and said, "You run pretty good…like a little mare I once had," and he gave a gentle laugh.

Rachel was nearly lost in the pain, but the comment seemed strange because it was spoken in clear English by a man that looked like an Indian. She said, "You talk like my husband." then closed her eyes again. Jacob reached forward and patted Rachel gently and said to Little Fawn in Wyandot, "She will live to be as old as you are."

"Brother, you are the only one who is old here!"

Giggling was heard at the rear of the lodge as Night-Bird-Singing listened to the familiar banter the two elderly people shared.

Jacob said, "Only the wise get old."

Jacob stood and pointed a bony finger at his niece. "You'll be old some day." This didn't stem his niece's giggling at all, and Little Fawn joined the merriment with hearty laughter as Jacob left the lodge.

Little Fawn returned her attention to Rachel. She combed the hair from the young woman's face and tied it back, so it would not bother her when she moved her head. She knew that Rachel would need something to eat. She told Night-Bird-Singing to put a pot of water on to boil. Little Fawn put dried beans into the water. Potatoes, squirrel and venison were added and the stew filled the lodge with wonderful smells. Corn was pounded into meal and corn cakes were placed near the fire to bake. A small pot of water was put on the fire for Jacob's tea. This was one habit he picked up, while living with the white people at the mission school. Over the years, the rest of the family had found that they enjoyed it as well.

. . .

Jacob walked slowly toward the large longhouse where the council was to meet. Other warriors and elders were also heading toward the building. Yellow-Hand was talking to a group of men in the shadows of a lodge. Several men spoke to Jacob as he passed and he stopped to speak to one or two of them.

Jacob paused before entering the longhouse as though he suddenly remembered something. Turning, he walked to the edge of the village and then another hundred yards to a different kind of lodge; it made of logs with a peaked roof. Jacob tapped on the board door with the tips of his fingers and the voice of a white man said, "Enter." Jacob reached for the door, but it was opened before he could touch the latch string.

The door was opened by a middle-aged white man dressed in a stained white shirt under a brown waistcoat and buckskin pants that looked as though they had been in use most of the man's adult life. They were slick with grease and black with dirt. His gray hair was tied back with a piece of silk ribbon, and a pair of iron-rimmed glasses were pushed up on his forehead. Jacob greeted him and entered.

A very small fire was burning in the fireplace and the flickering light reflected off a smooth bore trade rifle hanging from two wooden pegs just over the man's bed. A leather hunting bag and powder horn hung on another peg within easy reach. The white man had a pot of tea brewing and a kettle of meat and beans boiling. The cabin was about eight by ten feet. A small shed that held the man's trade goods. On a small rough table, a candle lantern cast light on the pages of a little Bible. A tiny ribbon marked the pages he'd been reading.

Jacob said, "Sutton, there may be white blood spilled in this village. I do not know whether it will be the female prisoner's or yours. If she can be saved, she will be my niece - but then you will be in danger. Warriors from this village have been killed. A cry is heard from the living for vengeance. The spirits of the dead cry for restitution. If they cannot have her... you are the whitest man they know. Old friend, you must go now while the council is in session. War makes things bad and many young men will look at you and see only a white face and they will see your stores as a chance for plunder. They will forget to pay their debts by honest labor and hope to escape those debts by your death. You have many friends here but we will not be able to save you."

Benjamin Sutton thought only a moment. He knew Jacob was right. He moved to begin packing.

He stuffed his journal and worn ledger into saddle bags. Then he closed the Bible to pack it too, but stopped and opened it again and took a nearby pen and ink and on the blank page at the front he scribbled —to Jacob L. Otter, from B. Sutton - The Bible was lovingly folded into a leather bag, and handed to Jacob. Sutton held the Indian's hand with clear affection and said, "With these pages we have shared many happy hours together. We have discussed the message contained in this book. We have discussed politics, science, and many other subjects. I have learned much from you. Jacob, I want you to have this little Bible. When you read it, think of what we have talked about and the many hours we have spent together, and know that we will do it again."

They clasped each other's left hand, knowing that this was a sign of trust and brotherhood. The normal hand for a weapon was the right hand and holding left hands allowed the right hand to remain dangerous: but trusted friends could always have their weapon hand free.

Jacob said, "I must go now, council has started…and you must go." Jacob turned and left the cabin and disappeared into the darkness with the leather pouch tied tight around the little Bible.

Sutton listened several minutes for any sound that would indicate someone had followed Jacob. Then he started packing. In half an hour he had loaded his pack horses with all that he could carry. The reason he had reached middle age as a trader was his honesty, fairness and understanding of the people he traded with. Sutton figured he had at least until morning before he was discovered missing. By the time a party could be organized to catch him, it would be late morning or early afternoon. He would have time to cache his trade goods and put some distance between him and anyone wanting his scalp. He couldn't help but think that he was getting too old for this foolishness. He knew this was only temporary. Things could settle down shortly and he could be back in business by fall.

Sutton tied the lead rope of his pack horse to the tail of the other horse and led them away from the village. He'd found a cave the year before and it spooked most of the Indians. He realized the Indians knew about it, but was sure they did not know that he knew about it. He was sure they wouldn't think he would hide his goods so close to the village. Being free of their loads, he could move very fast. Moving fast was important.

· · ·

Jacob had returned to the village and entered the longhouse. His entry was not noticed. Everyone was involved in smoking their pipes, talking to each other and watching the elders take their positions around the council fire that was located in the center of the longhouse. The interior was filled with haze from the council fire and the smoke of the pipes.

Yellow-Hand and others argued for blood for a long time. Then Pipe stood and addressed the council and the murmur of voices became quiet. Pipe said, "The blood of my warriors cries from the ground, calling for the revenge, demanding the life of that woman. Blood for blood."

Pipe then went to Kitcheogeemaw and handed him a small string of wampum before he took his seat on the bearskin. Others around the council nodded their agreement. Then Kitcheogeemaw stood and displayed several strings of wampum. He said: "This word is on its way to you."

He held up one of the strings of wampum. "This is to wipe away the tears from your eyes."

He took another strand, and said, "This is to remove the anger from your heart and open your ears so that you might hear my words. My warriors went out under the protection of my medicine; all my warriors returned. Our purpose was to honor the request of our mother who asked us to return the spirit of her daughter who died in childbirth. This woman holds the spirit of her daughter and grandchild.

He made sure he had everyone's attention, speaking quietly to make them hold their breath so they could hear. Then he asked them questions to make his point.

"Is it fitting and right that you consider our sister's spirit as payment for the blood of her brethren? We went to return the spirit of our sister, and with the Great Spirit's protection our mother's children were returned. Can you take these gifts and burn them to satisfy the cries of blood?"

Kitcheogeemaw indicated a pile of property, lying near the council fire.

"My heart is good; I speak the truth; may these gifts cover your dead."

Pipe stood up to respond

"My eyes clearly see that it was the intention of the Great Spirit to give us back our sister, we know this because he has also given back the spirit of your mother's lost grandchild. Vengeance will be made with the blood of our enemies, not the blood of our sister. She may live in peace."

It was over. Kitcheogeemaw's sister was safe.

Yellow-Hand and three other warriors stomped out of the longhouse in disgust. Jacob knew that he did the right thing in warning Sutton of the potential danger. Yellow-Hand had never been able to accept any decision that went against his wishes. Jacob also knew his family must be on guard. It would take the rest of the night for Yellow-Hand to work the warriors into a frame of mind to bring harm to Sutton. Jacob thought his friend would be well away by now.

Kitcheogeemaw stayed to talk to Pipe and two of his warriors. As Jacob passed them, he gave Kitcheogeemaw a squeeze on the arm and a smile. Kitcheogeemaw nodded politely and Jacob left the council and headed toward his sister's lodge with the good news.

By the time Jacob had greeted several elders on his way back to the lodge Rachel was moving with more ease. She was dressed in some of Night-Bird-Singing's old clothing, and sitting by the fire with a bowl of food, eating it with a carved spoon. Little Fawn was sitting on one side of her, Night-Bird-Singing on the other. Little Fawn was showing Rachel a bag decorated beautifully with dyed quills. Jacob heard Little Fawn ask him about the decision of the council — but it was not often that Jacob had news Little Fawn didn't already know, so he was making the best of this opportunity. After all, he must act the part of an elder and not show childish excitement.

Jacob sat down on the other side of the fire and reached for his pipe bag. He cleaned the pipe and measured a bowl full of tobacco very carefully and slowly. He put the pipe stem into his mouth and immediately Little Fawn held out a hot coal for him to light the pipe: She knew he would not speak until the pipe was lit and he had taken several puffs. He thanked her for her thoughtfulness, bent forward and touched the tobacco to the hot coal, then took several draws until the smoke was thick around his head. Jacob sat tall again, coughed, and puffed on the pipe for a minute or two until Little Fawn could stand it no longer. She said, "Brother, if you have something to say to your older sister, you had better speak NOW!"

"Sister.... old sister, this is your daughter...she carries your grandchild."

Little Fawn showed both surprise and pleasure, then concern as she thought of the punishment Rachel had suffered running the gauntlet. She hugged Rachel, who winced in pain. Little Fawn stepped back when she saw she had caused her pain and patted her face very tenderly as she would a child. Then Little Fawn placed her hands on Rachel's stomach and talked soothingly in Wyandot. She saw that Rachel didn't understand what was being said, and so she turned to Jacob and asked the English word for baby. Jacob told her and Little Fawn said very tenderly, "Ba-bee" as she touched Rachel's stomach again. Rachel nodded her head, knowing that this woman had nothing but tenderness in her for her and her unborn child.

Little Fawn went to the bags Jacob used earlier to make the medicine, and sorted through them until she found the one she was looking for. She removed the quantity she needed and started mixing them together in a stone bowl hollowed out for such a purpose. Meanwhile Jacob imposed on Rachel, pronouncing the name Catches-The-Wind in Wyandot and then in English while pointing at Rachel. Trying to imitate Jacob's Wyandot, Rachel said, "Catches-The-Wind" in Wyandot, then in English. Then she asked "Why do you call me that? What are you talking about?"

Jacob explained in English to Rachel. "White people would consider you adopted. You are now Little Fawn's daughter, Night-Bird-Singing's sister, and my niece." Jacob pointed to the woman and himself as he explained this.

Rachel asked, "How do you know English?"

Jacob became very serious. He didn't like talking of this part of his life. He said, "I'll tell you about that some time."

Little Fawn returned and started to pull the shirt away from Rachel's stomach. Rachel was feeling good enough now to be embarrassed and tried to cover herself. Little Fawn told Jacob to explain to Rachel what she was trying to do - and then to leave.

Jacob told Rachel that Little Fawn was going to apply an ointment to help her carry the baby with less sickness and pain. It must be applied every day. Jacob than said, "I am leaving; this old woman is going to put the medicine on you; you need to get well. There is a feast you must be ready for." At that Jacob got up and moved toward the door of the lodge. He paused and looked with affection at his family and turned to leave. Little Fawn pulled the clothing away from Rachel's stomach, this time there was no resistance as her new mother applied the soothing ointment.

Each day Rachel felt better under the tender care of Little Fawn and Night-Bird-Singing. Rachel became familiar with other women in the family, such as Strong Woman, who was Kitcheogeemaw's wife. Strong Woman's children were constantly in and out of Little Fawn's lodge. There was always a smile, a bit of food, a piece of maple sugar or a hug for the children.

Oddly, this happiness that surrounded her also made Rachel despondent: She missed her home and John. She knew that John would not give up on getting her back as long as he knew she was not dead. She wondered if he was safe. Would she ever see him again?

Time passed easily as she healed. One afternoon Night-Bird-Singing and Rachel were in a secluded spot on the bank of a gentle creek. They were not alone: Kitcheogeemaw lingered within sight. It was not safe for any woman to be alone without a guardian. Night-Bird-Singing was combing Rachel's wet hair. It felt so good to be clean again. Footsteps were heard among the leaves along the path leading to the two women. Rachel hurriedly adjusted her clothing so it would cover her and not bother the wounds on her back. Old Jacob came into view and asked her how she felt. Rachel told him she was fine. He pulled the collar of the shirt away from her neck and peered at Rachel's back, and said, "You heal quickly." Then he said to the girls, "Come." And he led them up the path to the village.

As they approached the village, Rachel realized that she was the object of the Indians' attention. The people smiled when they saw her and spoke to others behind them who were out of sight in the lodges. The children were in their best clothing. Excitement was in the air. Sounds of drums were heard and as Jacob led the two women into their lodge, a lone Indian male voice was heard in the distance singing a beautiful Indian melody. To Rachel, it sounded much like a lullaby. The interior of the lodge was full of people. The women stepped forward and gathered around Rachel. Little Fawn disrobed her after Jacob departed and the women dressed her in beautiful new clothes from head to toe. Night-Bird-Singing placed a silver hair plate in her hair, while Little Fawn painted Rachel's face. Little Fawn then pierced Rachel's ears and inserted ear rings in each ear. The singing outside continued. Little Fawn went to the food that was cooking over the fire and filled a bowl which she brought back to Rachel. As Rachel started eating, the rest of the women gathered around the food and started serving the men who came into the in the lodge. After the men ate they fed the children and then themselves. Some of the women were touching Rachel's clothing and talking soothing words to her in Wyandot. Little Fawn was telling everyone about the virtues of her daughter and her expected grandchild. She told of how good the Great Spirit had been to her. Now she had her daughter back, and a grandchild as well. Rachel did not know what Little Fawn was saying, but with the looks that were being directed toward her, she knew this conversation was about her.

Rachel saw Night-Bird-Singing in the huddle of people and smiled at her but got no reaction in return. Night-Bird-Singing looked down, then left her bowl of food and hurried out of the lodge. Rachel was very puzzled by this reaction and wondered what was wrong. Would she never be able to understand these people?

Her thoughts were interrupted by Jacob coming up to her and placing his hands on her shoulders. He said, "Welcome home Catches the Wind."

CHAPTER FIFTEEN

In front of Tom's cabin within the little fort, John and Nemesis were mounted on their horses, each holding the lead rope of a pack horse. Tom, his arm wrapped in a sling, stood near John's horse stroking its neck. Tom's wife, Catherine, was standing back so the men could speak freely with one another. John said to Tom, "If my place doesn't sell, keep it for what I owe you on these trade goods. We'll settle any difference when I get back. I just want to thank you again for all you've done."

"Don't worry, John. I just hope you have better luck heading to Johnson's than we did trying to catch them savages. I would go with you but now that Michael's gone, there will be more work than Catherine and I can handle."

Involuntary tears appeared in Tom's eyes and he attempted to hide them by blinking until at last he gave up and wiped the sleeve of his good arm across his face. "You just get Rachel back and we'll worry about money later. Catherine stepped forward and grabbed each of the men's hands. "I'm praying for your safe journey," she told them. Then the two men rode out of the confines of the little station and down to the fording place by the river. They stopped to give the horses a drink before heading into the forest.

Nemesis asked, "This Johnson up in the Iroquois country; do you think he has enough power to get Rachel back?"

"William Johnson has more influence with the Indians than any man on this continent; especially among the Iroquois. And the Iroquois have more power than any others. They reign over many tribes."

"What about your friends, Weiser, or Croghan?"

"They will help. I intend to find Rachel if I have to ask the King of England himself to help me."

"Well, I ain't the King of England but I'll do all I can to help you. I can shoot and track."

"Nem, you are my good friend and I tell you this . . . together we will get your wife back to you . . .and mine back to me."

When the horses were watered they began their journey to the north. Nemesis' horse slowed as the trail narrowed where it entered the forest, and he dropped in behind the pack horse John was leading. The quiet of the woods surrounded them. Nothing was heard but the clopping of the horses' hooves. This trail led to Town Creek, where they would pick up the warriors' path used by the Iroquois when they were traveling to and from their raids on the southern tribes.

It was nearly dark when the two men camped. John hobbled the horses and told Nemesis he would take a quick look to see if there was any sign of Indians and get some seasoned firewood at the same time. Nemesis busied himself in securing the packs. There was enough grass to keep the horses content, and the water would keep them near camp. They could get an early start in the morning.

Catherine had packed some food for their journey: corn muffins, a hunk of roasted venison and a pot full of her apple crisp covered with maple sugar. They made a small fire with wood that would barely smoke and in a short while both men were eating and drinking hot tea. John liked tea. Nemesis asked John if he had ever had a drink called coffee. John said, "Once, in Philadelphia . . . but that is a woman's drink. It's so bitter you have to use as much sugar as coffee to be able to drink it. Why, you can't even see through it. I'll stick with a man's drink. Nem, you can't go wrong sticking to what you know is good for ya."

As the darkness closed in on the isolated camp, the little fire cast wiggling shadows of the men onto the trunks of the trees behind them. The men finished their meal and brought out their pipes. Conversation stopped as they filled their pipes and lit them. As they replenished the tea in their mugs John said that when they reached William Johnson's, he was going to send Weiser and Croghan letters requesting their help in locating Rachel. Then, as the night wore on, they talked of old times. Memories were relived as the earth turned and stars appeared to travel across the sky. The fire died and they reached for blankets to wrap up in for the night. Conversation ceased as sleep overcame them.

An unrecognizable sound woke both men and with a start. They both rolled out of their blankets and reached for their rifles before realizing that the perceived danger was from John's ten-year-old mare. Standing between the sleeping men the horse was snorting into the ashes of the campfire. She was looking for salt, or a handout. Nem said, "We been snuck up on by a 600 pound, salt-hungry heathen with hard sole shoes." This brought a laugh from John and as the two men stretched, scratched and finished waking up.

When it was just starting to get light a bird flickered from tree branch to tree branch in the dampness of the morning, and a squirrel barked at the bird's intrusion on his search for breakfast. John and Nemesis decided to get started and have a cold corn muffin and a slice of venison as they traveled. Within a short time, the horses were saddled, the pack-horses loaded, and they were on the path. John told Nemesis they should make it to Hunters Station by the next night. In a few days they could be north of the Pennsylvania Colony and into the New York Colony, then they would be facing the same danger from different tribes.

The two men crossed into the Pennsylvania Colony and headed in a northerly direction along the base of Tussy Mountain. They passed some cabins that appeared to be abandoned. One had been visited by Indians; they could see several sets of tracks around it and a corner of the cabin was charred by fire. John and Nemesis figured there had been about 12 to 15 Indians in the war party. They appeared to have gathered at the edge of the cornfield before leaving and had left a great number of moccasin tracks in the tilled dirt.

Camp was not made that night until just at dark. No other signs of Indians had been seen and they decided to build a small fire since it couldn't be seen for more than a few yards through the thick undergrowth. They had traveled without a break since morning and wanted something hot to drink. They did without fresh meat because they were afraid the sound of a gunshot would bring unwanted guests to their camp. Jerky and the remainder of the corn muffins was their meal.

Before turning in, they put their rifles under their blankets and wore their hunting bags and horns. Both men lay quiet, each lost in his own thoughts. A whippoorwill was heard while frogs croaking in the distance. The sound of mosquitoes buzzing provided background music for the night symphony. Tinkling sounds of the small bells on the hobbled horses were heard as they grazed just out of range of the light of the small fire. After a few minutes of silence, John said, "Nem, it's hard to believe that not long ago all was right with me. I had a home, a good woman and a baby on the way. A man couldn't be happier. Now Rachel is gone and Joshua is dead. He was the first white man I met when I came out here in '42. There was not but three of us out here then: Tom and Josh and me."

Suddenly they realized the night sounds had stopped, all was quiet, even the bells the horses were wearing had stopped, which meant the horses had their attention riveted on something near them.

Nemesis reacted first, whispered to John, "Get out! Indians!"

John and Nemesis threw off their blankets and each rolled away and got to his feet on the run. Too late…a gun went off, then two more shots were fired and the camp was peppered with swan shot. Both men were hit. Nemesis lost his grip on his gun and grabbed his arm as he rolled deeper into the darkness. More shots were fired at John and he was hit and down.

Nemesis gained his feet and was up and running without his rifle but was still wearing the bag and powder horn. John was back up; he jumped into the darkness with his unfired rifle still clutched in his hand. Yips and yells filled the camp behind them. Nemesis and John heard nothing but their own footsteps and hard breathing as they fled.

The trade goods they left behind as they fled were a distraction for the war party and the warriors chasing John and Nemesis gave up quickly and returned to the camp to make sure that they got their share of spoils. The Indians caught the horses, loaded their new property on them, and led them westward.

John ran until the burning in his chest and loss of blood forced him to stop. He lay down in the deep shadow of a huge fallen tree trunk to listen for the sound of pursuing footsteps. He heard no one and after several minutes, when his breathing calmed, took stock of his condition. His arm was burning and he could feel several wet holes in his flesh where he had been pierced by swan shot. His sleeve was wet with blood. He had only one moccasin, no hat, and his powder horn had been torn loose from his bag some time during his run, so he had only the charge in his rifle. He had no idea where Nemesis was . . . if he had even gotten away. He needed to rest.

It was daylight when he awoke. He couldn't get his bearings and decided to find the creek where they had camped the night before then follow it up to Hunters Station. He did not know how far he had run, but knew that as long as he headed east he would hit the creek some time.

Some distance to the east, Nemesis was sitting under a tree next to the creek. He was wounded, though not as badly as John. Nemesis had several small shot in his back left shoulder and the back of his left upper arm. Most of the shot had gone through and out his arm. When he ran from the camp, he headed toward the creek. He had crossed it, ran upstream, reentered the creek and let the current take him back downstream. He floated along until he came to some thick undergrowth, where he crawled in and lay down until daylight.

When daylight came, Nemesis tried to clean his wounds and find something to eat. He shook the powder horn. The powder was still dry. He was glad to have such a well-made horn. He knew someday he would brag about soaking in water half the night but still keeping his powder dry. Hungry, he cut a small sapling to make a fish gig. He split one end into several prongs. These he sharpened and forced a piece of wood between each prong to spread them into a fan-like shape. Then he used his clasp knife to whittle small barbs on each prong, so a fish would not wiggle off before he could retrieve it.

Nemesis wondered what had happened to John, but knew that if it were possible to escape John would do it. He decided he would return to last night's campsite and try to pick up John's trail. If John had eluded the Indians, he would probably head for Hunters Station, but he didn't know what shape John was in. He could be lying wounded or dead somewhere. Nemesis knew that he had to do some searching before heading to Hunters Station.

Looking for John and for food he walked along the edge of the creek, peering into the shallow pools that might contain fish and into the woods for John or his tracks. Nemesis did not hear the sound of a twig snapping. But he did hear the next sound: the familiar voice of John coming from the trees and saying saying, "Nem, one of these days that belly of yours is going to get you killed."

"Sure am glad to see you in one piece," said Nemesis.

"Same here, Friend."

Together they sat down and after telling each other about their night. They leaned back against the tree and sat in silence for several minutes watching the water trickle by. Both men were exhausted. John had a bloody swollen foot, and the clothing of both men was covered in dried blood and dirt; their hair was matted with the dirt and mud.

Nemesis said, "You know…I didn't think Indians attacked at night."

John erupted in laughter, and Nemesis joined in. Trying to keep the laughter quiet made them laugh even harder. They stopped only when the exertion of laughing brought pain to their wounds.

When it was safe they took off their shirts and rinsed as much dirt from them as possible. They tore bandages from their long shirt tails, and made poultices of smart weed to ward off infection. Nemesis applied the green gobs of the crushed leaves to John's wounds, and John applied the same medicine to Nemesis' wounds. Makeshift bandages held them in place. John cut away the top part of his leggings and fashioned a moccasin for his bare foot. Nemesis went back to his fishing and in a little while he had several fish on the bank.

They peeled the outer bark off a standing dead pine sapling and took some of the dried crumbly interior for tinder. They put that in the flash pan of John's rifle, plugged the touch hole of the barrel with a small twig to prevent the unwanted firing of the charged the barrel, and then flashed the lock. The shower of sparks started several small glowing embers. They placed this against a handful of shredded poplar bark and a couple breaths started a blaze. In seconds, the small twigs, placed under the leaves, were burning and in minutes a good cooking fire was blazing. Soon both men were eating roasted fish.

As they ate they tried to decide what was next. John said, "Well, they got the horses and all my trade goods. We have one rifle, and you didn't lose your powder horn. But we don't dare fire a shot around here without drawing a bunch of them down on us."

Nemesis asked, "We still going to the settlements?"

"Yes, I'm not giving up. There are people I can go to for help. I'll do anything it takes even if I have to beg. Hunters Station is where we have to go first. He'll help us as much as he can."

Nem said, "Let's get started and get away from the smoke smell from this fire."

He got up, reached out his hand and pulled John to his feet. John grimaced with the sudden pain of movement. Stepping out he said, "In our condition it will take us at least two days to get there." John handed Nemesis his rifle and used the fish gig as a staff to help him walk. Both men hobbled on bruised feet down the creek toward the settlements.

CHAPTER SIXTEEN

Early morning rays of the sun were just touching the tiny blades of grass peaking up through the dirt of Joshua's grave. A crude stone engraved with his name and "1755" stood at the head of the mound of raw dirt. Down the hill from the grave, the pleasant sound of trickling creek water could be heard as it passed by Tom's quiet frontier fort. This had been one of Joshua's favorite spots. When he watched this station during Indian troubles, Joshua always circled the fort at dawn checking for any sign of intrusion during the night. Then he would be seen sitting on this hill watching the far mountain tops to the west. He would spend days just watching; protecting the families of this valley.

Lewis clutched his toy rifle as he lay next to the grave, faint salt tracks told the tale of tears that had dried on his cheeks. This time of day was the hardest for Lewis. Memories of that terrible day flooded his mind each morning when he awoke. Ben came to lick the salt away. Lewis grabbed the pup and spoke to him as if he could understand.

"Joshua was like my pap, Ben; I know he loved me even if he never said it…. I know he was wrong about the Indians too. He said not to hate. He was wrong, Ben. I swear to you that when I get big, I'm going to hunt and kill Indians. Nothing will make me stop, and you are going to help me. You and me will hunt them. They will pay for Joshua and ma and pap…. They were all wrong cause…cause dead Indians can't hurt nobody…can't hurt no one I love." Lewis cried into the soft fur of the puppy. He didn't like to cry. He didn't want anyone to see him cry.

Suddenly he heard Catherine calling him from inside the fort walls. "Lewis!…Lewis!…Lewis Hughes!…Are you out there again?" She peaked out through the gate and saw Lewis sitting on the ground next to Joshua's grave. "Come on in, son; it's too dangerous for you to be out there." She waited while Lewis got to his feet and walked back to the fort. They walked back inside the fort together.

Tom was standing just inside the gate. He put his arm on Lewis' shoulder, then stooped down to be on the little boy's eye level. He said, "I know you miss Josh, we all do, but he wouldn't want you to put yourself in the same danger that killed him. He loved you like a son and the best thing you can do for Josh is to grow up to be the best man you can be. Catherine and I worry about you when we can't find you, and you know the scouts haven't checked out there yet."

"I ain't afraid of no injun."

Tom knew that there was no reasoning with Lewis. "Catherine has breakfast ready. Go wash up, and we'll talk about this later."

Tom turned to look at Joshua's grave, then stared off into the distance. Michael's grave was a few yards past Joshua's. As his eyes lost focus in the sky above the grave he could see Michael as a little boy dragging in a big turkey he shot on their first hunt together....he could see him as a young man helping him build the trading post. He was a good boy that grew into a good man, but Tom couldn't remember only a boy or a man. He remembered them all together; the boy as a man and the man as a boy.

Tom let his breakfast get cold and walked over to Michael's grave and bowed his head for a few moments. He looked around at the other graves on the hill, graves of long gone friends, who died from the scalping knife and tomahawk, disease, cold, injuries, drowning, and just plain loneliness and hardships of frontier life. Two tiny graves held babies he and Catherine had lost; one only a few months old, the other just under two years. He thought how many marks life leaves. He thought that in a few years these marks of life would merely be rocks with names on them. It wasn't that people would forget. They couldn't forget what they never knew. Instead, it was simply a matter of death cheating the following generations out of the privilege of knowing. Death cheats knowledge.

Two young woodsmen leaving the fort to go on patrol called a greeting to Tom and brought his mind back to the present. Tom turned toward them and said, "If you get near the Phares place, take a look around it and let me know if I need to get by there in the next few days." The men nodded. One said, "OK, Captain Tom, we'll check it for you'. Catherine let us top off our horns with some of that fresh powder you got in the other day. We're going to try to get some meat tomorrow if we don't see fresh Indian sign."

Tom waved them off, telling them to be careful and not to take any chances. He walked to the open gate and passed through it, the moment with Michael was gone.

CHAPTER SEVENTEEN

Far to the north and east Nemesis and John approached a small frontier fort. Smoke hung heavy in the air. The two men exchanged knowing looks and cautiously walked the final few yards that would bring them to their destination. But the fort was burnt.

Cows, hogs and a horse lay dead, bristling with arrows. Bodies lay scattered and naked near the ruins, mutilated and filled with arrows. John and Nemesis wandered through the ruins, searching for signs of life. Nemesis had wandered to where a black man lay. In a few minutes John joined him. Death made them tired.

Indicating the black man's body Nemesis said, "A slave... I'd rather die like a deer. Deer at least run free and have a chance with getting away. Slaves are like steers, fed and taken care of but never free. This poor soul never knew what it was like to be like a deer...."

Both men stood in silence for a moment. These past weeks had melded the minds of the two men. John knew it wasn't deer or himself that Nem was thinking about.

"We'll get her free, Nem, we'll...your wife will know what it feels like to be like a deer...."

After a moment, he continued, "Must be the same war party that hit us; they didn't leave anything behind and nobody alive. I found Mr. Hunter over there." He pointed to a burned out cabin.

Neither of them had the strength, or the heart, to bury a dozen people so they picked up a piece of blanket and a torn coat to cover their own nakedness. John handed Nemesis the coat and said, "Let's get out of here."

Nemesis said, "We're going to have to stay off the paths till we find some place that ain't been burned."

"Good thinking, we're in no shape to take chances."

Supper that night and the next consisted of rabbits and squirrels they managed to catch with some well-placed snares. It had been two days since the fish dinner and fresh meat was a feast for appetites so long unsatisfied.

Several days later, shortly after sunrise, the tired, bearded, and footsore John and Nemesis approached the first settlement they had seen since leaving Hunters Station. John was carrying his rifle. Nemesis had only his shooting pouch and tomahawk. Both were wearing rags for clothing. They had discarded the remains of their moccasins and were barefooted.

This settlement was well established and far enough away from the frontier to be out of danger from small war parties. There were a lot of wagons, carts, horses, cattle, sheep, hogs and other animals around the tavern at the edge of the little town. Most of the animals were in corrals that the tavern maintained for the travelers. Early morning was in full swing with wood being chopped and split, fires smoking, food being prepared, the sounds of the animals being fed and the sounds of the animals wanting to be fed. Subdued voices of adults were heard from tents and canvas-covered wagons as people planned their day and tended to children. Some of the camps looked old. These people had fled the frontier due to the Indian scare. The needed refuge and this was the first place where they could find rest.

John said, "We made it, Nem, but I'm whipped. Now, if we can find someone I know around here, I can get a line of credit and we'll be alright."

The two men entered the tavern. The interior was dark. Several drunks, wagoners, and pack train drovers had never stopped their all night drunk; some were still playing cards. The odor of stale tobacco, whiskey and dirty sweaty bodies hit the two men as they entered.

A sweaty woman was at the fireplace. Two young boys carrying a large bucket of water pushed past with "by you leave, sir". John and Nem hesitated in the doorway, waiting for their eyes and nostrils to adjust to the interior of the tavern. The boys carried the bucket of water to a large iron pot that was hanging at the fireplace, poured it in, and swung the pot over the fire.

After waiting to be noticed by someone John finally yelled for service. A stocky, balding, middle-aged man with long greasy gray hair tied in a queue came to them. He was wearing a dirt-stained shirt, knee breeches and wooden shoes. He set a plate of bread and cheese on a tray near John and Nemesis then yelled at one of the boys to take it to the Squire's room. The tavern keeper finally took notice of John and Nemesis. "Ain't seen you around here before. You want something?"

He eyed Nemesis with a look of suspicion.

John said, "Is Mr. Alexander Butler about?"

"Ain't seen him in a while. Don't know when he'll be back either."

"Do you know where he is now?"

A look of disgust crossed the man's face as he looked the two men up and down. He decided he was too busy to talk to the common trash John and Nemesis seemed to be. They were dressed like beggars and poor ones at that. He walked away, calling back to them over his shoulder, "He's gone to Baltimore." In a louder voice, he yelled, "Boy, I told you to get that tray up to the Squire's room. Now….and don't forget his tea!"

John and Nemesis turned to go.

One of the drunks suddenly noticed John's fine rifle and thought it looked out of place in the hands of a man dressed in such shabby clothes. He called to John, "Hey, fellow, you lost?" His friends laughed and egged him on. "Do you own that boy there?"

John responded, "No one owns him; he is a free man."

"Has he got papers?"

John didn't answer. Another drunk joined in. "Didn't you hear my friend?" …. Does that boy got papers?"

John answered in anger. "If he did, you wouldn't be able to read them…He's a free man."

"You calling us ignorant?"

Nemesis was trying to pull John out the door, whispering "John, don't start nothing. They're drunk and looking for trouble. Let's just leave." A stoneware mug came flying through air, hit John's head and broke, splashing Nemesis with ale. John went down, bleeding from a scalp wound. The drunks were on Nemesis in a flash. Still thinking they might be able to get away if he slowed these men down a little, he hit the first one so hard the man didn't even wiggle when he hit the floor. The second man fell under Nem's iron fists, falling into two others. The tavern keeper came running and yelled for them to break it up. He grabbed the plate out of the hands of the boy who had just picked up the platter of food for the Squire, and shoved him toward the door. "Go get the sheriff!" Just as Nemesis was about to haul John out the door The tavern keeper pulled a pistol from behind the bar and hollered for him to stop. Then he yelled toward a backroom, "Netty, bring the big gun! Hurry!" Thinking they had free reign to whip Nemesis, some of the rough men moved toward him. The tavern keeper fired the pistol over the heads of the assailants. The burning gun powder made contact with the combatants' necks and faces, and the noise of the pistol got their attention.

"You ain't makin' a mess of my place."

The men turned toward the tavern keeper. One said to his friends, "His gun's empty now, let's get him too." As they started toward the tavern keeper, Netty stepped into view. The large black woman had a calm unshaking grip on a double gun. Her disinterested face made the rowdy drunks believe she could handle any situation she had a mind to. She said flatly, "Mine ain't empty." Netty handed the large bore double barrel flintlock gun over to the tavern keeper, and all the combatants became very docile. The tavern keeper said, "We'll all just calm down and wait for the sheriff. He'll be here any minute."

Both John and Nemesis were on the floor. Nemesis had taken a few hits but was mainly bending down attempting to check on the still groggy John. In a few minutes the door opened and the sheriff and a few interested citizens entered. The sheriff was a big man wearing a burgundy colored waist coat. A brace of brass pistols were held in a finger woven sash tied around his waist. Several of the drunks started to talk at once. One said, "We caught them for you, Sheriff, they tried to get away but we stopped 'em. That one has to be an escaped slave, and nobody looks like that other man without being a looter, just look at that fancy gun he has; he's taken it from somebody." A hat-less man with a bruise already swelling his eye closed said, "They started it. That slave don't have no papers." A voice slurred advice, "Lock 'em up, Sheriff. Respectable people like us can't even walk the streets any more." "They was trying to get away," said another, then pointing to John he continued, ". . . that one broke my mug."

The sheriff hollered for them to be quiet or everybody would be put in irons and they would have to stay there until the magistrate made the circuit next month. The room got quiet and the sheriff bent over and looked at John and Nemesis. Addressing two citizens he said, "Put these two in irons, we'll find out what their story is and who they are."

One of the men left and soon returned with shackles and began clamping them on Nemesis. Nemesis reluctantly held his hands out to have them bolted on his wrists. Another set was placed on his ankles. Nemesis had experienced shackles before, a long time before, when he was a boy. He despised the memory of seeing his mother taken by one man and the rest of his family by another. He despised the iron around his wrists and ankles now, but he submitted because wisdom told him this was not the time to fight.

The sheriff asked the tavern keeper, "Did you see what happened?" The tavern keeper answered, "I didn't see nothing. I heard a ruckus and they was into it. I don't know who started it. I just want to be paid for what they broke up."

The sheriff turned to the remaining rowdy, smelly, fighters who didn't have sense to slip away while the shackles were being fetched and spoke to them. "When you people are about, there's always trouble and you are never at fault. You'll spend time in the stocks yet. One of these days somebody will see you do something and I will be around."

The Sheriff's comrades jerked Nemesis to his feet and shoved him out the door, while another finished placing shackles on John's wrists and ankles. He was still incoherent and had to be carried. A cart belonging to one of the curious spectators was sitting at the front of the tavern. The men put John in the bed of the cart and told Nemesis to climb in. The cart's owner protested but the sheriff told him to drive it over to the jail and the township would give him six pence for the use of it. The cart's owner happily climbed up next to the makeshift guards and the group headed toward the jail. The ride was short, but by the time the slow-moving ox had pulled its load to the jail, John was thinking clearly once more.

The guard took Nemesis and John around to the side of the jail. A sour-faced old man brought a bucket of water and some rags and told them to get cleaned up. Nemesis made a bandage for John's head from what was left of his shirt. When they had cleaned up as best they could, the guards directed them inside.

The sheriff wrote down their names and other personal information. He said he had to hold them until he could verify the information by contacting Tom Thomas. John and Nemesis were taken to a hall room where the shackles were removed. The sour-faced old man appeared again and made it clear that they were his as long as they were there. He impressed this upon them by slapping them across their legs with a stick.

They were taken to the back part of the building and pushed into a small dark cell. There was straw on the floor for a bed, but no blankets, only fleas and lice. The cell had one small window with iron bars, and a wooden bucket sitting in the corner.

Pain seemed to cover John's body much more completely than his tattered clothing. There seemed to be no place that didn't hurt; not even the soles of his feet were free of aching. His wounds started bleeding again, but at least the blood was seeping rather slowly instead of flowing. Nemesis sat in the dim light of the small room, and leaned back against the wall. He didn't say anything. The daylight was strong outside now but John was so tired he didn't want to move. Sleep would be welcome. John looked at Nemesis and couldn't remember seeing him so completely defeated.

John heard sounds coming from outside the window and when he looked through it he saw an enclosed area. The large room looked like a temporary log addition. Light sliced through the unchinked logs and dim light touched John's face at the same time foul smells reached his nose. The light that illuminated his own fingers as they gripped the flat iron bars also revealed the presence of occupants in the other room — Indians.

John was confused. What were Indians doing here? Fatigue pulled him away from the window and his eyes searched the dimness for a place to lay down. A voice from outside stopped him.

"Hello, John Phares."

John drove his body to lift him back to the window once again. Looking through the bars he tried to see who was talking. As his eyes adjusted he recognized a tattooed old warrior looking at him through the window.

"Turtle Man!"

"I was once Turtle Man, now I am Michael," said the Indian.

John went closer to the window. "Turtle Man...er...Michael . . .You cannot know how glad my heart is to see your face once more. It has been a long time...Why are you here? Why are you called Michael? Who are these people?"

The old man laughed. "Should I answer quickly all your fast questions, or will you stay long enough so I can answer well?"

"...Ahhhh, take your time, I will be here long enough."

Michael began to talk as he pulled a clay pipe and tobacco from a pouch and prepared to smoke. He took his time. John knew he could wait, though he could barely stand. He addressed the old Indian, telling him he was injured and asked if the old man would be insulted if he sat down. The old man, pleased to see so much respect once again, said "Sit down my friend". When the pipe had burned its fragrant smoke into the air Michael began to talk in broken English with a heavy Lenapi accent.

"I am a Christian now, John Phares. The Moravians missionaries taught us the great message and changed our lives. In our village we went to meetings and planted corn and made things for white people to use, like baskets and brooms and canoes. We made money and lived like white people. Our relatives became mad with us and made fun of us. They leave."

The old man paused. John could tell he was saddened by the divide. Then he continued.

"When war come, our angry relatives come to us to get food to eat. We feed them because it is right…besides if we not help maybe they kill us. They bring fighters who are not our relatives. Not all warriors are our relatives. White people learn that fighters stay in our village. White people mad because they think we help what relatives do. Some white people want to hurt us, but some white people know we love Jesus and try to help us. They say we should live here for our own good because bad white men want to kill us… We come to this place, but now I not feel like they do us favor."

John heard strength return to his voice as he calmly continued the clear and concise description of their situation. "We cannot fight our relatives because we love them as our Lord teach us. We cannot talk to white men because they do not listen. We are to love all men Christ say…. I tell you, John Phares, this is much harder to do than to fight."

Nemesis had been listening and said, "I know that."

Michael continued, "These people with me here in this strong lodge are my brothers and sisters in Christ. A few I was related to before, but now they are my same spirit."

Michael held out his arms so he could see his tattoos and scars. "This skin is old, but I am new. These marks that cannot be rubbed off are all that is left of the warrior you knew. My heart is clean. The hate is gone. I was captured by Jesus Christ and do not speak of the old man; of hate and killing. Now I like to talk of love and peace, instead of war and hate. I tell you, John Phares, people more like to hear about war and fight."

"You don't fight any one?"

"I fight hate, John Phares. If I hurt any man, it make hate. Hate lead to trouble and it hurt him who hate, maybe more than one who is hated. It make anger in heart, stop love from growing. It is all a strong warrior can do to fight hate…"

John was silent, as he thought of the words of this man who was once a most feared warrior. Michael had tattoos on his face and upon his forehead representing over 30 scalps he had taken. The tattoo of a speaker of his tribe was on his throat, the tattoo of a snake was on the left side of his face, and the tattoo of the sun was on the right side of his face half encircling his ear. He had scars covering his entire body, representing dozens of battles he had participated in, both by himself and as a member of war parties. He had been the leader of the most secret and honored warrior society in the Delaware nation. The name "Turtle Man" was most honored. The turtle was the animal that his nation believed the earth was founded upon. John understood what Michael had been. He was truly amazed at this man's insight regarding what it meant to be a Christian, and most of all, the peace within him. He was impressed that this man would turn his back on a lifetime of earthly honor, so he could face a Lord of love that he'd never seen with his eyes. He was successful in everything men valued, but he valued Jesus more.

Finally, John spoke. "You are truly right, Michael; It is all a warrior can do to fight hate. You strengthen me my friend. Thank you."

"You rest, John Phares. You are good trader man. You good friend to us."

John forced his legs to lift him once again to the little window. Peering into the other room he asked, "Michael, have you heard anything about a woman who was captured by the Wyandots? A pretty woman…my wife. She was captured when the leaves were new, along a creek near the waters of the Cohongoronto."

Michael reached up to touch John's fingers at the edge of the tiny window and looked up at him, then shook his head no. "You rest, John Phares. The Great Spirit will watch over your woman."

John sagged to the floor once again.

Michael moved away and sat on a blanket on the floor; he began singing a part of an old hymn he had learned at the meetings: "I'll bear the toil, endure the pain, supported by Thy Word…"

Nemesis was sitting in the corner of the cell wrapping himself in what was left of the filthy tattered blanket they had found at the burned out fort. John crawled over and found a place to lie down. Getting as comfortable as possible, he said to Nemesis. "There are a whole lot of white people who should be grateful that Turtle Man is now Michael." Exhaustion and the darkness of the night closed around them and they both fell into a restless slumber.

CHAPTER EIGHTEEN

Michael

When John awakened he had no idea how long they had slept. Maybe a day. Maybe only a few hours. He would still be asleep if loud voices hadn't wakened him. Nemesis was already awake and standing at the peep hole in the jail door, trying to see what was going on. It was dark but flickering light could be seen down the hall and through the window where the Indians were held captive. Firelight glowed through the unchinked logs. John asked Nemesis what was going on.

"I don't know. There are a lot of men…." He was interrupted by a loud crash and the building seemed to tremble slightly. John moved stiffly to the window to look out. The light, now brighter in the Indian quarters than anywhere else, revealed Indians waking up and afraid…except Michael, who was standing between the group of Indians and the torch bearers at the door. A man's voice was heard from the shadows beyond exclaiming, "They're in here."

John yelled, "What's going on out there?"

The same voice spoke to others, "There's more in that room over there."

Footsteps were heard outside. John and Nemesis moved toward the door as light got brighter and the footsteps closer. A crash against the door made John and Nemesis step away from it. A human form appeared in the opening of the door.

The man held a candle lantern up so light filled the tiny room. He called out, "They're not Indians! It's just a couple of drunks." A voice from down the hall responded, "Then let them alone and get over here!"

The man left and John and Nemesis went back to the opening and yelled out, "What are you doing?"

The faces of two more men appeared and one of them said, "What do you think we're doing? We're killing Indians for a change."

John answered, "These people didn't hurt anyone."

"What are you, some kind of pious fool? These singing sons of hell helped the scum that butchered my wife and babies."

The words were like blood-smell to a hungry wolf. A mass of armed people pushed through the door of the Indians' cell. They started dragging Indians out into the night. First they took men.

While several armed men stood watch, the remaining Indians huddled around Michael and started to sing in the Delaware language. The Indian men, mostly old men, were stone faced. The women sobbed, but they all continued singing. Then the words became broken English. The melody was familiar. They were singing hymns. The Indians' turned their eyes upon one another and would not look at the armed men. The hard faces of the remaining Indian men softened as they looked upon their wives, daughters, children, grandchildren and brothers and sisters. Their eyes shimmered out their love for one another as their voices praised their Lord. Outside the singing was caught in the hearts of the Indians that were already taken away and they joined in songs with those who sat inside. The singing outside was interrupted with thuds and involuntary grunts. The blows that were bringing death were covered over with angry German, Scottish, and English accents. Slowly, gradually the singing outside stopped. The angry voices became louder again as they returned for the Indians who remained.

Guns, knives, tomahawks and clubs filled the hands of the men with angry voices. One man carried a massive hammer made of a portion of tree trunk with a long hickory handle. It was a tool very familiar to John. It was used to drive posts into the ground. Candlelight and pitchy, smokey, torches provided light that contrasted sharply with the darkness that held them aloft.

The Indians continued singing and made no fight except to struggle to cling together as the small huddle was forced outside. Now John could not see anything except an empty room. All the light was outside now and the room was lifeless. Nemesis crowded his face against Johns to see why the singing had been moved outside. Nothing but shadows. Shadows of men's legs arms and angry heads stretched into the room from outside, covered the floor and climbed the log wall. The shadows were moving, over-sized, giant, fast, and silent. All the sounds were outside. Singing. Crying. Anger.

John and Nemesis felt pain no more. Their wounds were forgotten. Their muscles could not ache. Nothing they ever saw had made them forget their own body like this night did. Even in all his years of slavery, Nem had never seen such anger, violence, or killing. John thought he and Nem would not have forgotten all about their arms and legs and breath so completely if they were not chained, imprisoned, and powerless. They would have fought. But they were like the deer that ceases to struggle even as it is being eaten alive by a panther. John always wondered how the deer could seem so detached from its own death. Now he knew. Something greater than his own mortal life was happening. Something beyond the control of physical creatures. Death was happening. Death was celebrating.

John and Nemesis were men of violence and they lived in a violent world. They knew the sounds that came from outside. They knew thumps and crunching sounds as skulls were broken. But they had never known those sounds to come from bodies that were not trying to kill them and the people they loved. Not from forms that sang and bowed before them. Not from children, women, old men, and submissive men. Not from weak, young, soft, peaceful bodies. Voices in the crowd shouted about "how easy it was to kill Indians this way" and that "it was about time some of the bloody heathens paid for the misery they were causing."

The singing continued but the mob seemed to have calmed. Their angry voices dropped more and more as the hymns the Indians sang were offered up by fewer voices. With horror John and Nemesis realized that even the sounds of the children had decreased. Only two or three little frightened voices could be heard. With this realization they found their own voices. John and Nemesis were only voices. All the rest of them was imprisoned, but they had their voices.

John and Nemesis tried to reason with the mob as torch light flickered on the prison logs amid the shadows of death. John screamed hoarsely, "They are innocent! You bastards! Stop!" Then almost as in prayer, he said, "Please stop!"

A white man appeared at the cell door. He aimed a pistol at John and said, "You better shut up, you ignorant, pious, Indian loving, son of a female dog. I'll blow your head off. Between people like you and Quakers and missionaries, the Injuns will kill us all before…" His reason seemed to fail him, and his words failed him, so he became loud, "JUST SHUT UP."

John stepped back with Nemesis. The Indians were still singing. John and Nemesis recognized the words of the old hymn, "A Mighty Fortress is our God", even though it was being sung in broken Delaware. "…and tho this world, with devils filled, should threaten to undo us, we will not fear, for

God hath willed his truth to triumph through us." John looked into the eyes of the man pointing the pistol at him; then raised his chin and began to sing along with the surviving Indians. "The price of darkness grim, we tremble not for him, his rage we can endure, for lo his doom is sure, one little word shall fell him."

The sound of John's voice affected the shadows that moved on the walls in the other room. The man with the pistol could no longer look John in the eye and lowered the muzzle. Nemesis joined John in singing with his rich baritone voice. The sounds of death had slowed but still continued outside. Tears shimmered in John's eyes. Nemesis and John both looked into the dim face of the shamed man as they continued to sing. With the pistol lowered they could see how young he was. A scar ran from the corner of his mouth to his ear, pulling a deep distorting trough of shadow across whiskers that were still soft as a child's. Another scar furrowed through the skin beneath his hairline. Then he too bowed his head and moved into the shadows.

The Indian voices continued to be silenced. Now only Michael was singing. A moment later, his voice stopped as John and Nemesis heard the sound of a dull sickening thump. But John and Nemesis continued to sing as tears now fell freely from their cheeks into the dust on the prison floor. "The whole body they may kill, God's truth abideth still. His kingdom is forever."

The light from the torches melted away with the sounds of the murderers' footsteps. Darkness filled the walls as the little lights the crowd carried were taken away. In the silence, Nemesis put an arm around John and bowing his head, he whispered, "Amen...." The two men stood together in the empty cell, grieving for humanity in silence.

CHAPTER NINETEEN

Wyandot Summer Village

Rachel's back was bothering her; she had been hoeing all morning in knee-high corn. She straightened up and walked over to where several children and women were sitting in the shade of a huge old oak tree, and sat down. The cool breeze felt good as the sweat dried on her face and neck. The past weeks had been a series of adjustments for her, but she was learning a few words of Wyandot and making friends.

Strong-Woman was the overseer of labor this year. In order for the women to enjoy each other's company, they all worked in one field at a time, or at whatever job they may have to do. One woman was acknowledged to be in charge each year. When she accepted the honor the rest of the women bound themselves to obey her.

When planting time arrived, the women assembled in the morning and went to the first field. Each woman took one row to plant and then they proceeded to the next field and so on, until they had planted the fields of the whole tribe. If there were fields not completely planted, they would come back to that field and finish. By following this method, jealously of one having done more work, or more harvest, than her neighbor was avoided. It was easier to share the fruit of labor that had been shared. Underpinning their cooperation was the knowledge that they worked for survival rather than profit. As comfortable as they lived by the labor of women, the Wyandot people knew their survival was a fragile and uncertain thing. They had seen hunger. They knew starvation.

Beyond the village, there were huge fields of fruit trees, more than Rachel had ever seen. The village also had many fields of beans and squash, as well as corn. Joshua had told her stories of these fields. He said that many years ago he had visited the tribes in that area. They always had large supplies of fruits, and the corn grew higher than he had ever seen any white man grow it. He said he had seen ears of corn as much as two feet in length. Rachel thought he was telling her a story. She wished now that she could tell him she believed his words.

Little Fawn touched her shoulder interrupting her thoughts. She offered Rachel a drink from a pot of water. Rachel reached for it and thanked her. Rachel could see Night-Bird-Singing laughing and talking with a group of women as they were hoeing the corn. Night-Bird-Singing was still avoiding Rachel as much as possible. This had been going on since the adoption ceremony. Rachel was greatly bothered by Night-Bird-Singing's attitude, but she could do nothing about it. She couldn't speak the language fluently enough to make herself understood. When she asked Jacob about it, he said Night-Bird-Singing "was jealous."

Nothing would be said about resting while others worked, but the other women had certain looks for anyone who took too much time. This usually was enough to get the message across. Rachel picked up her short-handled hoe, and headed back into the hot sun. She retraced her steps to the row of corn where she had been working, and started chopping weeds and loosening the dirt between the corn plants. The woman in the row next to her looked up and smiled. Rachel was not lazy and the women who had been working next to her these past weeks knew that. The sun rose and the afternoon grew hotter as the women toiled in the field. Night-Bird-Singing broke out in a song and the rest of the women joined in. This made the work go faster.

Every once in a while, someone would tell a joke while they worked in the fields. Sometimes it was at the expense of a warrior who saw himself as a ladies' man. All the women would laugh, and this encouraged more stories and laughter. The gossip of the village was discussed, the corn was hoed, and the long day came to an end. Before the women left the field, Strong-Woman told them where they would work the next morning, and the group headed back to their husbands and the many more chores that must be performed before they could think of rest.

CHAPTER TWENTY

Jail Cell - Lancaster, Pennsylvania

John was shivering with a fever. He coughed and pulled the tattered blanket around him. For the past two days he had been incoherent. He believed Joshua was in the cell with him and Nemesis, and got very upset when he wouldn't talk to him. He talked to Joshua and called for Rachel and carried on conversations with her. A smile would come on his face as he heard her voice, but these periods always ended with John calling to Rachel, "I'm sorry... I'm sorry"

Nemesis tried to keep the bullet hole wounds clean and allowed them to drain each day. He asked the jailer to bring him some smart weed but the old man only laughed and said that the world would be better off with one less troublemaker. The only help Nemesis could get for John was a bucket of water once a day. He wiped the sweat from him when he was burning up and wrapped him in the blanket when he was shivering. He changed him when he soiled himself, which wasn't often because he didn't drink enough water. Nemesis was afraid that John would not last more than another day or two.

He had just finished cleaning John's wounds again when he heard the clatter of a heavy keys and some voices coming toward the cell. He recognized one of the voices. It was Tom's. He spoke to John, "He's here . . . Tom's here. You just hang on; you'll be alright now. TOM! We're in here!" he yelled. As the jailer was fumbling for the key to unlock the cell, he was saying, "We thought he was one of them scavengers, what with him having that fine gun and all. Most everyone is gone out of the back country for fear of Injuns. There is some low life scum that go in and take what they please. We figured that was how these boys come to git shot. You understand, don't you?"

Tom was upset about the suffering his friends had to endure in the jail. He greeted Nemesis, then moved to check on John. He said to the jailer, "I take it you don't feed your prisoners or make provisions to keep them healthy."

"Well, sir, this place is overrun with people from the frontier and there is little enough food to feed them, let alone vermin like this…I mean like we thought these…we just thought…well, you understand."

Tom glared at the jailer who stepped back out of reach. Tom turned back to help John. He wrapped his coat around John and said to Nemesis, "How long has he been like this? Are you alright?"

"I'm alright. He's been like this since the night after they killed all them Indians. Ask Mr. Jailer here about that mess!"

"No need, the word is all over. The brave men of this country should be proud."

The jailer said, "I didn't do nothin'. Those men would have killed me if I tried to stop them…I told them not to do it."

John seemed to be aware of Tom's presence and what was going on. Tom said to him, "John…hey…can you stand to eat one of Catherine's good meals, or do you want to stay here?" John smiled, then started coughing. Tom and Nemesis helped him up and started toward the cell door. But the jailer stepped in their way. He nodded his head toward Nemesis and said to Tom, "I can't let that boy go. He ain't got no papers to prove he's free. You can take this here other fellow but…."

Tom had had enough, and turned to the jailer. "This ain't no boy. Here is a better man than anyone I run into around here. I bought him and signed the papers to tell any government that he is free man. Tom put his face in inches from the jailer's eyes. "If I have to show you papers to prove it, I will, but you will truly regret putting me to the trouble…."

The jailer's nerve had left him. He was not accustomed to dealing with a man like Tom and he said, looking at Nemesis, "Alright…you can go…. I'll tell the sheriff I saw the papers." Tom held his place right in front of the jailer's face and he didn't blink an eye. The jailer was afraid to look him in the face and afraid not to. Tom said, "Sir."

The jailer was confused. He responded, "What?"

Tom answered, "Tell this free man, you can go … Sir."

The jailer laughed a nervous laugh, thinking Tom was joking, but then realized he was not. He meekly complied. Tom didn't smile. Nemesis shook his head wondering how many more friends Tom was going to make for him. Together Tom and Nemesis supported John as they left the cell. Tom had the jailer bring John's rifle to him.

Outside a riding horse and a horse-drawn cart were waiting. They helped John into the cart, then Tom handed Nemesis a pouch of biscuits and cheese, along with a bottle of whiskey. Nemesis put a blanket over John and then handed him some food. Tom mounted his horse and rode forward leading the cart horse. Slowly they left the crowded refugee-filled village and headed back to the frontier.

. . .

Many days later Lewis was the first to see Tom and the others approaching the fort. He started yelling, "Tom's here! They're here! They're here!" Little Ben sensed Lewis' excitement and began barking and jumping around. No one seemed to mind the drizzling rain that had been falling.

For days, Lewis had been sneaking away from his studies and chores so he could watch for Tom and the others. He was afraid the Indians would get them. Before leaving, Tom had told Lewis how long it took to get to Lancaster, and how long it would take to get back. He made sure he calculated the additional time it would take because he had to avoid the overrun settlements and travel through towns that were strong enough to resist the warriors. And to avoid the English military that confiscated every animal it could find. He even added three days in case of trouble. But Lewis was sure they were several days overdue. The boy had almost given up.

The people in the fort heard Lewis yelling, and several men ran out to meet the trio. Lewis and Ben were first to reach the cart. Lewis saw John half propped against a pile of straw with a wet blanket around him, shivering. He was almost hysterical as he asked Tom, "Did the Indians shoot him? Is he going to die?"

"He'll be alright, Lewis. Calm down. He's pretty sick though. Go tell Catherine to get dry clothes and a warm bed ready for him. Hurry now…and tell her to get out her doctorin' stuff." Lewis ran off.

By the time the cart pulled up in front of Tom's cabin, it was surrounded by neighbors and friends. They helped a cold and stiff Nemesis with a very sick John Phares out of the cart and inside the cabin. Catherine gave orders to anyone who happened to be close by. She hugged Tom first, and moved over to John to feel for fever and carefully checked him as his wet clothing was being removed. When she was done with her examination Tom asked,

"Well, how is he?"

"He would be in better shape if you'd have made camp and not rode in the rain."

"We couldn't make camp the last couple of days, woman! There ain't hardly a cabin standing. The war parties are thick. I figured it best to push on. We only had this one wet day. He was pretty good till the rain hit."

Catherine turned to one of the women by the fireplace and said, "Get me a pot of hot water and a pot of cold...." To Tom she said, "You get out of them wet clothes before you end up like John here." Tom moved to obey while Catherine examined John more carefully. Nemesis moved to the fire and started taking off his wet shirt. Tom handed him a blanket. Lewis came in as Nemesis was removing his shirt and he saw the wounds on his back. Lewis asked, "Is that buckshot holes, Nem?" Nemesis nodded.

Catherine came over and began to probe the wounds on Nemesis. "John has them kind of holes, but yours are healing up. There is still some lead in there that will have to come out." I'll be sorry to dig open a half healed wound." Nemesis winced as Catherine examined the wounds, then she backed off, put the blanket around his shoulders, and told him to finish getting the wet clothes off and get dry. She moved back over to John.

Nemesis told Catherine that the buckshot had been working its way out of both of them the last week or so, but Catherine flatly replied, "The rest of those shot are going to have to be taken out so we can get rid of that badness that will just come and go if we don't." Nemesis pulled up a chair in front of the fireplace and sat down, letting the warmth from the fire penetrate the coldness that he felt clear to his bones. Tom left the room to change into dry clothes. Lewis was squatting next to Nemesis, watching him and thinking very seriously about something. "Nem, did you kill any of them? Did you make 'em pay?"

"No, we was too busy runnin'. We was just layin' there almost asleep and all of a sudden they was on top of us, guns going off, yelling, hooten and hollering. Why it was enough to scare a body half to death. We just took off."

Lewis was disappointed and mad at the same time. "I can't wait to get big enough. He pulled a knife from his sheath. "I'm going to scalp Indians till there ain't none left to scalp."

Catherine looked at Lewis. The boy seemed fixated on learning everything about Indians so he could know how to find them. She couldn't seem to break through to make him understand that a boy his age should be playing and having fun. She couldn't give up, but she had retreated a little: Now she just tried to keep him from expressing his passion. "Lewis, you know what I told you about using that kind of language in my house . . .and put that knife away. "

Nem reached out and rested his big hand on Lewis's small shoulder. "Lewis, I know you're mad but don't always be worryin' about Indians all the time." Lewis looked over at the unconscious John, as Catherine worked a small lead shot from one of the holes, and said, "Indians kill everyone I love. It don't matter who it is. I can't love no one no more Nem."

Nemesis said, "Awwww now, you mean you don't love ol' Nem here?"

Lewis was confused. Sure he loved Nem, but was afraid to show it or admit it -for Nem's sake. Lewis said, "I can't Nem. If I loved you, them shots would have killed you. So it must be that I don't."

"Lewis, I want to tell you something. Death is surely goin' to get us all sooner or later. Don't you dare hold back from lovin' someone cause you're afraid what might happen…. Seems like the only way to cheat death is to love so hard that the one you love don't ever leave your heart. Joshua is still in your heart, ain't he?"

Lewis nodded his head slowly, almost painfully.

Nemesis continued, "If you hold back you'll only wish you hadn't. Love hard, boy, so you can always say you didn't hold back."

Lewis was torn and confused. He feared not so much for himself but for the terrible deaths his love seemed to cost people. He took one of Nemesis' huge fingers in his little hand and said,

"You don't know…. Can't you understand? I can't love you no more."

Nemesis attempted to pull Lewis to him to comfort him, but Lewis stiffened his body, though he could not fight the big man's strength he would not respond to the touch of a loving heart.

CHAPTER TWENTY ONE

Wyandot Village

The sounds of unfamiliar activity awakened Rachel. She got up, straightened her worn clothing and walked outside. She saw packs and bundles being made up. Then she remembered that Jacob said they would soon be moving to winter quarters. For the past few days there had been frost in the morning and leaves were starting their change. There was a freshness in the air that only the autumn brings.

Rachel saw Jacob moving toward her. He was smiling and greeting everyone he passed. He saw Rachel watching him and an even broader smile broke out on his face as he walked up to her. He rubbed his hands together and stuck his chest out, inhaling the cool air. He said, "Ahhhh, winter camp…hunting…trapping…it's the time of the year for real men."

"I didn't know you hunted."

"I don't. I sit in the lodge and tell stories to the children." Then he laughed and walked off.

Little Fawn called to Rachel and told her to start bundling up the bedding; there was no time for play today. Little Fawn was gathering supplies to take with them to winter camp. Kitcheogeemaw was talking to other men while Strong Woman supervised the older children in her lodge; everyone prepared for the journey to winter camp.

Since the adoption ceremony, Night-Bird-Singing had not associated with Rachel. At times, she was even threatening. Once she had pushed Rachel to the ground when they found themselves alone working in the cornfield. She stood over Rachel with a heavy stick, drawing it back as though to hit her, to hurt the baby. Just at that moment, Little Fawn approached the field and called for the two girls. Rachel knew that Little Fawn had prevented certain harm. She avoided Night-Bird-Singing as much as possible after that. She stayed close to Strong Woman when working in the fields, and tried to be with other women when she was away from the lodge. She could feel the coldness of Night-Bird-Singing's stare many times during family activities. On this day, there was too much to do; she could not dwell on unpleasant things. Rachel went back into the lodge and rolled up each person's sleeping mat, and tied the bear and deer hides into bundles.

The family would be traveling by water in dugouts and canoes, so it was essential that everything be kept dry. Little Fawn supervised the loading of the family's possessions. Rachel, Night-Bird-Singing and one of Strong Woman's children carried the bundles to the dugout they would use.

Other families were shoving off and saying their goodbyes while those standing on shore waved and sent their blessings and good will toward them. Each family was traveling to its own winter hunting grounds. It would be a long time before they saw one another again.

By late morning everything was loaded, and Little Fawn and Strong Woman's families were soon heading north and west into a completely uninhabited area. Kitcheogemaw poled the dugout and his father-in-law, Crane, poled the canoe. Rachel experienced a wave of loneliness as she realized she was traveling even further away from John.

The travelers kept their canoes on the shady side of the river as the sun traveled across the sky. The afternoon became almost hot, but the coolness of autumn would come with evening. The insects buzzed and the fish jumped as they fed on the unfortunate bugs that landed in the water. The children and old people dozed as the two canoes gently rocked back and forth with the exertion of the men who poled upstream.

Rachel leaned back against some bundles and before she knew it, she was asleep. Then, John was standing at the foot of the bed shaking it and saying, "The sun's high and I got a hunger worked up. Let's get the day underway!" She felt so happy, but wondered what the sun was doing shining in her eyes through the cabin roof. She tried to get up to hug him....and was suddenly back in the dugout, trembling from waking up so fast. The sun was shining in her eyes through a break in the branches of the trees and the shaking of the bed in her dream was caused by Jacob moving around trying to get a more comfortable spot. She closed her eyes again, but the dream was gone.

Evening shadows covered the surface of the water as the canoes rounded a bend in the river. Kitcheogeemaw stopped poling and motioned for the other craft to stay back and be quiet. He stooped down and pushed the dugout nearer the river's bank. Quietly he told Crane that he saw a deer

108

about two bow shots up ahead. He told everyone to remain quiet for a few minutes while he got into position. Kitcheogeemaw wanted Crane to paddle toward the deer. If he got close enough, he was to take a shot at it. If the deer ran, Kitcheogeemaw would be waiting for it to pass him.

Kitcheogeemaw put on his hunting bag and powder horn. He grabbed his rifle and stepped out of the dugout then silently disappeared into the trees. Strong Woman's father readied his gun and laid it within easy reach. Crane paddled the canoe slowly around the bend. The dugout followed with Jacob doing the poling. The deer spotted them immediately, but stood where it was. He raised his head and pointed his nose high in the air, attempting to get a scent. Getting no indication of a scent at this distance, he stomped his feet. His tail came half-way up and he stomped his foot again. He took a step toward the approaching canoe and lowered his head. Suddenly he dashed into the woods just as Crane was about to touch off the shot that would have taken him.

A shot broke the quietness of the scene about a hundred yards into the forest. Crane picked up his gun again and watched the shoreline very closely in case the deer was only wounded and attempted to escape. When no deer appeared, he put the gun back down and everyone smiled. They knew that Kitcheogeemaw made a kill and they would have fresh meat.

The men poled the crafts toward shore, and everyone began setting up camp for the night. Strong Woman picked up a burden strap and headed into the forest to retrieve the deer's body.

In a few minutes, Kitcheogeemaw appeared. He took a pack to one side of the activity, sat down and started cleaning his rifle. Crane and the other men joined him while the women finished setting up camp; they wanted to hear Kitcheogeemaw tell about killing the deer.

Rachel and Little Fawn were busy pounding corn into meal and making small cakes by the time Strong Woman dragged the deer into camp. An iron pot half full of bear's fat was put on the fire and in a short while, pieces of fresh venison sliced into small chunks were dropped into the hot fat. Laughing and joking, everyone started spearing and eating pieces of meat and corn cakes until they were stuffed. The little that remained of the deer meat was cut into thin slices and spread over a rack. A small fire was kept under it all night to keep heat on the meat so it would become jerky by morning. The smoke would flavor the meat and keep the bugs away until it dried.

As darkness enfolded the small group of travelers, blankets were provided for everyone. The men brought out their pipes and lit them. The pleasant smell of tobacco smoke mixed with the scent of the campfire. The family gathered around the fire and relaxed in its glow, while some told stories of other times around other campfires. Then the singing began. Night-Bird-Singing had learned a French lullaby from Jacob when she was a little girl, and she started singing the words but stopped in mid-sentence and left the fire. Rachel thought she saw tears in her eyes as she turned to go. Everyone seemed to catch Night-Bird-Singing's sadness and this brought an end to the singing and good spirits around the fire. As it burned low, one by one, they wrapped themselves in their blankets and went to sleep.

Rachel lay for a long time listening to the night sounds and wondering what it was that troubled Night-Bird-Singing. She had been so loving those first few days. Why was she so angry now? Rachel decided she would ask Jacob the first chance she got. She smiled when she thought of Jacob. She saw a lot of John in him. He seemed to have no ill will toward anyone. The relaxation brought on by thoughts of Jacob sent her spiraling into sleep.

The next thing Rachel knew Kitcheogeemaw was calling for everyone to get up. It was just daylight enough to see and everything was covered with a light frost. The fire was built up and a pot of water was put on to boil for tea. The tea and leftover corn cakes made a quick breakfast, and after loading the canoe and dugout, they were soon on their way.

They continued traveling north by west, and finally several days later they came to an open beach area, pulled into shore and got out.

This time instead of unloading just those items needed for an overnight camp, everything was unloaded, and the two crafts were pulled up on the beach as far as possible. The men started digging a trench beside them. The women picked up the packs and began to walk up a path. Rachel was standing next to Jacob, struggling with a pack and asked him, "Aren't we staying here?"

"No, only the boats. We bury them to protect them from the winter."

Taking notice of her pack, he said, "You shouldn't be carrying that heavy pack, you're not used to it." He picked a bundle off of her pack. As Rachel was walking away, Jacob carried the bundle over and put it on top of Strong Woman's pack, and patted it. This was not noticed by anyone, including Strong Woman. She struggled to shoulder her pack and finally lifted it up on her back, then followed Rachel up the path. Smiling at his own wisdom,

Jacob walked over and picked up a small bundle in one hand. Humming and singing while he carried the little bundle and his walking stick, he brought up the rear behind Strong Woman. Kitcheogeemaw and Crane would catch up when they finished burying the dugout and canoe.

It was a cold cloudy day with rain threatening. After a couple of miles, they arrived at a good campsite on a rise of ground. Little Fawn had been in the lead since leaving the river, and had already laid a fire and was gathering wood by the time Rachel and Strong Woman reached the campsite. Night-Bird-Singing cut down several saplings and trimmed off the branches. A half-faced lean-to was made with the saplings by tying a sapling across two trees that were several yards apart. They laid the other saplings along the cross pole, then peeled bark from a large tree and laid it on the saplings, like huge overlapping shingles. The impending rain would be easily and completely blocked. Branches were laid on the ground inside the shelter, and leaves were piled on these to keep the family off the damp ground. With the fire burning in front of the shelter, and its warmth being reflected inside by several large stone, placed on three sides of the fire, they had a warm cozy camp. The women were nearly finished with a second shelter where they could store their bundles when Kitcheogeemaw and Crane arrived.

Over a meal of boiled corn seasoned with maple sugar, bear's oil and venison jerky, Rachel asked Jacob how much farther they had to travel to the winter camp, and when would they get there. He told her that if the rain would end by morning, they would get to the winter camp by the following night.

Rain started as a slow drizzle and built up to a steady downpour which lasted most of the night and turned to freezing rain before it stopped near dawn. The forest looked like a wonderland of sparkling diamonds when the sun rose. All of the trees were covered with a thin coating of ice and for the first hour on the trail, each step taken crunched into frozen grass and leaves. By mid-morning the sun had warmed and everyone was soaked from water dripping off the trees and bushes. They stopped when the sun was high and the path had dried. Everyone dried his feet and changed into dry moccasins. The wet moccasins were tied to their packs to dry as they continued on.

Toward evening they passed through a stand of pine trees and entered a meadow-like clearing with a stream running through it. Two weathered lodges with frames exposed to the weather came into sight. The women walked up to them and laid down their packs. Little Fawn approached one and shook it to check its sturdiness. She addressed Strong Woman and Night-Bird-Singing and said, "This needs to be replaced before we cover the lodge." She removed a tomahawk from her pack and started cutting a suitable sapling. Strong Woman continued checking the frames on both lodges.

As the rest of the family arrived, a flurry of activity took place and everyone pitched in to repair the lodges and organize the camp. The women soon had the frames repaired, and they unrolled some packs that were made up of loom woven mats. They placed the mats on the bare areas of the frame, added fresh peeled tree bark, and soon the lodges were ready for occupancy. Then the children and women started gathering wood for the fire. Rachel knew how to do this and pitched in. She made several trips taking dead branches and saplings to the camp; then she saw Night-Bird-Singing struggling with a dead sapling whose branches were caught in some bushes. Rachel wanted to help her pull the sapling free but Night-Bird-Singing gave her such an angry hateful look, that Rachel backed off and watched her drag it into camp alone. Then she turned and walked into the woods. Jacob had been watching and followed Rachel.

Rachel stopped at the foot of a huge tree, looking in the direction she thought was home. She began to cry and didn't hear Jacob come up behind her until he spoke her Indian name.

"Catches-The-Wind." She didn't answer. Jacob saw the tears on her face. He asked, "What are these for?" He touched her cheek with his finger.

"I…I'm just so lonesome." She looked away from Jacob and both of them stood quietly for a few moments. Then she asked, "Why doesn't Night-Bird-Singing like me?"

Jacob looked away from Rachel, then he seemed to make up his mind about something and said, "She had a husband, but he left her for a woman who could bare him children."

Rachel blurted out "She can't have babies!"

Jacob's voice was so soft Rachel almost couldn't hear him talking. "We all have our wounds…some are slow to heal." He placed his hand lightly on her shoulders as he said this.

Together they started to walk back to camp. Along the way Rachel put her hand in Jacobs as though she were a little girl. The evening shadows were falling and the glow of the fire in the lodge could be seen through the trees by the time they reached camp. The cold night air seemed almost warm to Jacob.

CHAPTER TWENTY TWO

Tom Thomas' Fort

John stepped out of the cabin with Lewis and the growing Lil' Ben. The trees were completely bare and a coldness was in the air. Autumn was losing its grip as winter pulled the world away from the sun. A cough was all that was left of John's illness. He buttoned his coat and tied a light scarf around his throat as they walked over to where Nemesis was working. Nemesis saw them coming and stopped banging on the hinge he was forging. He straightened up and said, "Well, it is good to see you up and about. I thought for a while that you were a goner, but old Saint Peter apparently has enough trouble without you."

John chuckled and started to respond but stopped at the sounds high above. All of them looked up as they were interrupted by the sound of honking wild geese in formation, flying south.

John said, "I never get tired of seeing that, and you're right; I thought I may not get to see it again. I never realized how much time has passed. I was sick for a long time. Why, it's comin' on winter."

Nemesis said, "Yes, and then spring and we can go see about Rachel again."

"Nem, I'm not waiting for spring."

"You ain't fit to go nowhere yet."

Something else was bothering Nemesis, other than John's health, and he said, "John, I got a good contract with the military. I'm going to have to set up shop at Fort Cumberland though. I can make enough by spring to buy Delly back, then I can go with you. I never figured you'd be well enough…."

John responded before Nemesis ate himself up with guilt. "I'm happy for you, Nem. Now don't you worry about me. You get that wife of yours back and stay with her. I'll be fine. Ain't as many war parties in winter, so it'll be safer. I might even make it all the way to William Johnson's this time."

"I'm sorry, John. I just didn't…"

"NEM, you are my friend. You know my heart. Don't you worry none 'cause soon Rachel will be here too, and we can celebrate. Okay?"

Lewis pulled at John's coat sleeve and said, "John, me an' Ben will go with you."

John bent down to the dog and said, "Is that right, Ben? You want to go?" A nearly grown Ben barked.

"See, John. He said yes."

John didn't want to disappoint the boy. He told him it would be awhile before he could go because he needed to build up his strength, but they could have some fun doing that. They must get some meat for the Thomas' for winter. He and Ben could help. John said, "Lewis, you get to bed early tonight, we'll go hunting tomorrow. There might be some of those geese we just saw down at the end of the cornfield at first light. We'll see if that fowling gun that I built for Tom last year works! Let's take Ben and see if he's any good at fetching geese!"

Lewis was excited. It would be his first hunt since Josh took him and he told John that he knew Ben would bring anything he sent him out for. Lewis spoke to Ben, "Come on, Ben, we're going to practice fetching geese!" They ran out the gate as the two men watched. John nodded toward the boy and said, "I better follow them, I need to walk anyway."

That night, John, Lewis and Ben slept on the floor in front of the fireplace so they wouldn't wake the rest of the household when they got up. But it happened that all three were awakened by Catherine stoking up the fire. She told Lewis to fetch a pot of water and let Ben out for a run. Soon Lewis and John were sitting in front of a hot bowl of boiled oats and maple sugar. Catherine smiled, but said nothing about them oversleeping. She just said, "You two be careful" as they went out the door.

Dawn was breaking as the two hunters stepped out into the frosty morning air. Lewis called for Ben and the three headed toward the gate. John called quietly to the sentry posted near the gate and they exchanged greetings. No sign of Indians had been seen in several weeks, and it had been quiet all night.

Ben walked ahead of Lewis and John as they followed the path to the cornfield. It was a path Ben had traveled many times, and he made several stops to sprinkle a stone or a tree. John watched Ben very carefully; if there was danger, Ben could be their only warning. The dog was young, but he was beginning to show his intelligence and sense.

As they entered the cornfield, John whispered for Lewis to call Ben to him and follow. Lewis snapped his fingers and whispered for the dog to "heel". Ben followed close behind Lewis as they started sneaking along the stacks of corn that resembled small wigwams in the early morning light. John stopped and whispered, "You can hear them feeding just over this rise. You hold Ben here and as soon as I shoot, you bring Ben and come running. I'm going to try to line up as many geese as I can before I shoot." Lewis nodded and took a good hold on Ben. John, on his hands and knees, started crawling from corn stack to corn stack. He reached the last one at the top of the little rise and saw over a hundred geese feeding. He watched them for several minutes until he got eight or ten lined up.

The geese started "honking", their sounds becoming quicker and quicker. John knew that was the prelude to their flying away. It was now or never. He pulled the hammer to full cock and stepped up into view. It froze the geese in front of him for just an instant. Others were taking off. The sound of the large caliber smooth bore going off in the stillness of the morning sounded like a cannon. The smoke was clearing as Lewis and Ben raced past John, one yelling, the other barking.

John and Lewis soon had 12 geese piled up. John looked toward the fort and saw Tom and several others walking toward them. "These feathers will sure feel warm sewed up in some pillow ticking, and I ain't had roast goose since last year," said Tom as he started picking up dead geese, tying their feet together and looping them on a pole. In a few minutes, he had geese on the pole and the pole on the shoulders of two strong young men. On the way back to the fort Tom said, "It sure would be nice to have some chestnuts to make dressing for these here geese."

John asked, "Lewis, do you want to pluck geese or pick chestnuts?"

"Pick chestnuts!"

Lewis and Ben turned off the trail and headed toward the stand of chestnut trees they were passing. John exchanged guns with Tom and followed Lewis and Ben. The path led down to a small stream where Lewis and John had to step from stone to stone and then jump to the other side of the stream to keep their feet dry. Once across they climbed the shoulder-high stream bank. Ben simply wadded through the water and met them on the bank. This was the only place in the bottom that was out of sight of the fort. As they started up hill, the hair on Ben's back stood up, and he started growling at something in the bushes about 40 yards away near the tree line. Instantly John said, "Indians, Lewis! Call Ben! Get into the stream and stay behind the bank. Then head to the fort and tell Tom. Now hurry!" John stood with his rifle at the ready, looking for any movement in the bushes. Lewis grabbed Ben and put a strap around his neck. He had to pull him before he would follow. John crouched behind the stream bank and watched the tree line as Lewis and Ben ran for help.

Movement! The Indians were trying to flank John. He saw a flash of color as one ran upstream and another downstream. John ducked down behind the bank, out of sight and moved upstream several yards, so they would not know just where he was. He hoped the boy was safely away. He had to hold his fire as long as he could. It was a deadly game: The Indians knew that the first one to charge him would be the first to die.

A voice from the bushes yelled, "Prisoner, prisoner!" But John had no desire to be a prisoner and did not answer. An answer would give his position away. He worked his way deeper into the bushes and looked back toward the fort. He could see Lewis and Ben just running through the gate. If he could keep the Indians at bay a few more minutes, help would be on its way.

From his new position, John could see the area he had just left. A painted warrior was crawling toward the edge of the bank. The Indian hesitated, listening, then suddenly jumped over the bank and into the stream with his tomahawk at the ready. Just as suddenly, he crouched against the bank when he didn't see John. If it hadn't been so dangerous John would have laughed.

John watched as the Indian looked for sign of tracks. The Indian looked upstream, trying to penetrate every bush and possible hiding place. John barely breathed when the savage stared at his hiding place. Then the Indian looked downstream. While he was looking away, John quickly looked upstream to see if he could locate the other Indian he knew was there somewhere. He didn't see him. He moved his rifle so the muzzle pointed at the Indian he was watching. Suddenly he saw the other Indian.

Neither Indian was aware of the presence of the other. The first warrior was under the bank near where they had first seen John. The second Indian began to sneak in that direction too. John placed a lead ball in his mouth and pulled the stopper from his powder horn and got ready to shoot.

John watched both warriors now. The second man moving carefully toward the first. Almost quicker than he could have imagined possible the second Indian moved. John was glad he did not have to fight the man for he was powerful and quick...In a flash the second Indian sprang over the bank and onto the back of the first savage, swinging his tomahawk as he jumped. He sank it into the head of his friend before he realized what had happened. A look of utter surprise came over the savage's face when he saw what he had done. He'd killed his fellow warrior thinking it was John. Woodsmen often dressed as Indians and even painted like they did. At Fort Bedford a few men painted all the same so they would know one another in the heat of battle. The big Indian looked up and down the bank and found himself alone with the body of the Indian he'd just killed.

John's shot ended his shock by blowing a hole in his skull.

John quickly closed the flintlock's frizzen, poured a charge of powder down the barrel of his rifle and spit the ball into the bore. The spittle caused a small amount of black powder to form a seal on the bullet as it went down the barrel. John thumped the rifle on the ground and the ball was seated against the main powder charge. The pan was primed and the gun ready to fire again. Some woodsmen reamed the priming hole large enough that the gun would prime itself with a slight thump for situations like this.

John quickly sighted on the tree line and gave a war whoop the rest of the Indians would recognize as a victory for him and defeat for them. The whoop from John and silence from their fellows would tell this war party that this was not an inexperienced settler they were fighting. Two rifles were fired at him from the tree line and war whoops were yelled in defiance from the wooded area.

Just then, bullets from the rifles of several militia started flying high over John's head toward the woods. The men were being led by Tom as they came running down the hill toward John's position. The savages gave a final whoop and retreated into the forest. This was just a small war party but with the loss of two warriors, John pitied the next white man they met up with. Their revenge would be terrible.

Tom came running up to John and after seeing John wasn't hurt, sent several men to scout the area and warn the rest of the valley of the presence of a war party. Tom couldn't believe that two Indians were killed with one shot. This was a story that would be told for generations to come. John tried to explain how it really happened, but no one wanted that explanation. It sounded better saying two Indians with one shot.

John took the tomahawk and knife from the first warrior and saved them for Lewis. These things would be his reward for his cool headedness, obedience, and bravery. The scalps were removed and taken along with the Indians' property, including the two rifles found in the tree line believed to have belonged to the dead Indians. Indians had no respect for a white man that did not scalp. To take a scalp is to take a prisoner for eternity. No Indian wanted to be a prisoner for any length of time. So scalps were taken in hopes it would prevent a return to a settlement where the power was so great and the white men fought like Indians. In the pouch belonging to the Indian John shot the men found a woman's scalp with long blond hair stained pink with her own blood.

John felt light headed and weak after this excitement. His coughing got worse and by that evening he was back in bed. Catherine wouldn't let anyone see him until the next day when he was feeling better. She made him drink a lot of herb tea and whiskey, so he had no trouble sleeping. When he woke up late the following morning, he felt like a new man and told her, "I'm tired of baby food; I want some of that goose meat I smell cooking." She laughed and said, "You must be feeling better because when you're sick, you're a whole lot easier to get along with. There's a lot of folks who want to see you when you're up to it. But you ain't getting' out of bed yet! You stay there; I'll get you something to eat."

Lewis, who had been waiting his chance, came in, carrying his tomahawk. He was followed by Ben. Lewis said, "John, you feeling alright? Me an' Ben have been worried about you."

John greeted Lewis with a man's handshake and made a fuss over Ben's alertness. "Lewis, Ben saved our lives. They would have had our scalps if he hadn't of smelled them. You got the best dog I ever saw." This praise made Lewis' face light up with pride as he hugged Ben's neck. Ben was nearly as big as Lewis now and still growing.

Footsteps were heard on the stairway and Tom entered the room. He asked John how he was feeling, but before John could answer Tom proceeded to tell him what the scouts found. He said, "They checked south to Fort Ashby and north to Cumberland, and it looks like them Indians were a part of a larger war party, maybe Killbuck's. At least that's what the word is at Fort Cumberland. They wiped out Fort Warden over near Cacapon four days ago and it looks like they split up into small parties after that. The same time you were having problems, Fort Nicholas was being hit just north of here. People there were not harmed much; there was nothing but just a bunch of shooting and hollering. A couple of people got hurt, but none killed.

A little distracted, he said, I'm going to ask Charles West and John Steeth to check on your place tomorrow when they go to Fort Cumberland. John didn't have much concern for his place anymore. If his place was burned, then it was just burned, and he would build another. He said, "Don't have them go out of their way to check on it." Tom assured him that it would be their decision. They had to pass right by his place and it would only be a few minutes' walk out of their way. Then he looked into Johns eyes to make sure he was listening." Those Indians that tried to ambush you were probably coming to the gunshot you made at the geese. If they had already been laying there watching this place, they would have taken you and Lewis when you passed them going out. As it was they missed you coming and going. They were still strung out when the first two came on you. You and Lewis were saved by the hand of Providence this morning.

The conversation was interrupted by Catherine's footsteps. She tried to be stern and fussed at Tom and Lewis for invading her patient's privacy, but her good nature showed through. As she set a plate of food down where John could reach it, she smiled at Lewis and said, "Time to go. You'll have time to visit again. He's going to mind me this time. He's not going any place for the next couple of weeks!" As he and Ben reluctantly moved to go she told Lewis to fill the wood box, wash for dinner and put that filthy tomahawk outside. She said, "We're having our big meal now instead of tonight... and be careful with that tomahawk!"

She addressed Tom and said, "If you want to eat with John I'll bring you a plate." John broke in, as lonesome as he had been for company, and said, "He does, don't you, Tom? And bring one for Lewis too; we can't leave my little partner out." Catherine lifted her eyebrows and told John to drink the tea while it was hot and she left the room. Lewis flashed John a big smile as he disappeared out the door after the wood.

When they were alone, John said, "Tom, I'm heading for William Johnson's next week. I have to try to get there before snow starts falling. Now don't tell Catherine because she'll just start fussing, but I can't lay here any longer and not do something to get her back." He paused. "Do you think I can get a horse for one of the guns we got from those Indians yesterday? I need even more than that. Any trade goods you can get for the rest of what those Indians had, or for the value of my farm, I'd appreciate."

Tom said, "John, I'll get what I can and you can draw what else you may need from the store house, so don't go worrying yourself about it. I agree with Catherine on you not going any place for a while, but I can understand how you feel."

Lewis came in with his arms full of firewood and left for another load as John said, "I'm going by myself. Mr. Johnson should have that letter you sent him by now and he may have some news by the time I get there."

. . .

Early one morning, a week later, John was securing a bundle to the saddle on his horse. Tom was standing nearby giving final advice as Catherine came out of the cabin. She walked over and handed John a large pouch of biscuits. She reached up and put a hand on his forehead and then his cheek and told him, "You don't have any fever now, but if you don't take care of yourself, you'll be on your back again in two days. I wish you would just forget this; you're not going to be doing Rachel any good killing yourself."

"Yes, Mrs. I'll take care of myself."

"You are just too bullheaded to listen to reason," she told him, then gave him a hug and buttoned the top button of his coat before returning to the cabin's porch. Tom advised John to stay away from the big forts because the Crown was impressing horses into service, since they needed every pack horse they could get their hands on. Tom said, "They been workin' em' to death and ruining the rest."

"I'll be careful."

Just then, Lewis stepped into view and stood next to Catherine. He had a bundle and his toy gun. He said, "We're ready, John."

This took John by surprise. He was at a loss of words. He didn't want to hurt Lewis but knowing the dangers and suffering this trip could bring about, he said, "Lewis, it's too dangerous. I'd like to take you with me, but look at what happened to Nem and me the last time."

"That's because Ben wasn't there; you need us!"

"Lewis, you stay here and take care of Tom and Catherine."

Lewis became very quiet. No one noticed the determined look on his face. Catherine put her arm around him as John mounted his horse. As he turned to go, snowflakes started falling from the dark clouds. John pulled the brim of his hat down.

Tom said, "You'll be in our prayers, John." John smiled, nodded his thanks, and rode away.

Tom stepped over to Catherine and put his arm around her waist. Catherine said, "I wish he did have someone to go with him." Both of them watched John until he was out of sight. Lewis had slipped unnoticed back into the cabin. He put several of the remaining biscuits and some pieces of jerky into his little pack, and laid it behind the door out of sight, then came back out on the porch to stand behind Tom and Catherine. When John was out of sight, they all turned to go about their daily routine. Catherine told Lewis to be sure his chores were done, then he could finish his school work while she did some needed sewing. Lewis secured Catherine's promise that he would be able to go outside after that, and he ran off to fill the wood box.

The chilly November sun was starting to break through the afternoon clouds as Lewis penned a simple note on his school slate, saying, "I am going with John." He then printed his name and placed the slate next to the candle lantern where it would be seen. Catherine was gone, helping Tom at the storehouse, and Lewis knew he had time to put several miles between himself and the fort before she returned. By the time they discovered the note, it would be too late for them to look for him that night. Lewis figured it was easier to leave the fort during the day. If he waited until night time, he and Ben might be seen by either the night guard or the by the other dogs.

Lewis put his pack on and started playing with Ben next to the open gate of the little fort. He threw a stick and sent Ben after it. In a little while, people didn't take any notice of him playing and he just walked off into the woods.

There had been no one on the trail since John had left early that morning, so Lewis had no trouble following John's tracks. It didn't take long for Ben to pick up on what Lewis was doing, and he started sniffing the tracks and the air above them. Eventually the large dog took over the lead. Lewis patted him and said, "Good boy; find John."

Lewis had spent a lot of time with Joshua on hunting trips and had learned how to take care of himself on the trail. As it grew dark, he found a tree that had fallen in some past storm, and cut several small saplings with his tomahawk, and laid them against the tree trunk, covering them with branches from a small pine tree. He piled more pine branches inside his little shelter and closed one end with branches.

Lewis shared some biscuits and jerky with Ben and both of them crawled

121

into the small brush shelter. Their shared body heat made it very cozy and soon both were sound asleep. Lewis was awakened by Ben moving to get out of the shelter. He looked out as Ben was making his rounds, sprinkling every tree trunk and stone he came to in the early light of dawn. Lewis followed him out and stretched, scratched and yawned a few times. Then he dug into his pack and broke a biscuit in half to share with Ben. Soon both were on their way, munching as they walked. They came to a stream and both had a drink; then found where John had crossed the day before and were on his trail again. They had been walking for a couple of hours when Ben started sniffing the air and gave a low growl as he looked back down the trail behind them. Lewis knew someone was coming. He found a place to get off the trail without leaving tracks. Ben followed Lewis to some thick bushes several yards off the trail and they crawled under them and lay watching the trail. Lewis petted Ben until he heard the sound of horses coming. He leaned close to Ben and told him to be quiet. They watched as Tom and one of the scouts from the fort rode by. In a few minutes Lewis and Ben fell in behind them. Lewis relied on Ben to warn him when the riders were returning.

A few hours later Ben's hair stood up on his back and he gave a growl as he caught the scent of the returning riders. Lewis and Ben hid again. Tom was talking as they rode past. "That boy learned well from Joshua. If he don't want to be found, he ain't gonna be. I know we've ridden right by him some place along here." The men rode on and Lewis and Ben wee soon on a clear trail to John.

CHAPTER TWENTY THREE

The only snow John had seen so far were the flurries that chilled him when he left Tom's place. He wanted to travel a few more miles before making camp, but when he came upon a deserted cabin, he changed his mind and decided to stop there for the night. It had been getting much colder the past few hours, and looked like snow would fall before the night was over. He thought it best to start out warm and dry in the morning. Catherine's advice made good sense: He had to keep his health if he wanted to do Rachel any good.

This cabin had a good roof and would keep him dry for the night. He scouted the area round the cabin but found no sign of any recent human activity. He returned to the cabin and checked the fireplace and chimney before making a fire. He soon had a pot of water heating for tea. As John unpacked his bed roll, a small bag that hung around his neck swung out from the opening in the neck line of his shirt. He paused and opened the bag and removed a lock of hair with a small piece of ribbon tied around it. He stared at it for a few moments, then gently replaced it in the pouch. Just as he put the bag back inside his shirt, he heard a noise outside the cabin. He quickly and quietly grabbed his rifle, checked the priming, then stepped back into a corner shadow. Moments went by and the tension mounted. Indians? No. Tom had told him to be on the lookout for Lewis. It was likely Lewis, but he'd better be sure.

The door moved slightly and John put tension on the trigger as he pulled the hammer back so it would not make any noise clicking as the sear was engaged in the flintlock. The door moved again. John aimed the rifle. Something hairy pushed the door open and stepped inside, Little Ben.

John whispered, "Ben!" He was relieved and uncocked the hammer and lowered the gun as Ben started wagging his tail, and then his whole body, as he greeted John. John knew Ben wasn't alone and looked out the door, but didn't see Lewis. He called quietly, "Lewis!" There was no answer. After a minute or two of looking through the dim forest in the approaching darkness of night, John went back into the cabin. He went over to the fire and put the grease pot on some hot coals. In a few minutes, he put a piece of meat in the pot and spooned some of the grease into a pan, and made some flour gravy, while the dog sat and licked its chops. When supper was ready, John spooned some into an old wooden bowl. He walked to the door and not too loudly called again, "Lewis!" The smell of cooking food and the second invitation did the trick. Lewis couldn't resist. He walked in sheepishly and John nodded to the bowl. Lewis grabbed it and ate ravenously.

John said, "It's been four days since I left; when was the last time you ate?"

Lewis answered, "Two days ago I had some food, but me and Ben ate more than I thought we would. But I didn't want to catch you too soon because you would just take me back." Lewis stopped gulping his food long enough to look at John and say, "You need us to help. Ben here can smell Indians in the dark; That's why I wasn't afraid...we can help."

John told him that he would leave him at the next station they came to, but Lewis already had an answer. "You left me at Tom's and it didn't do any good....and I'd just follow again. Long as Ben is with me, you can't get away from us."

John looked at Lewis for a minute, then acknowledged defeat. Tom could track a snail in a rainstorm and he hadn't found Lewis. He doubted anyone could stop the boy once his mind was set. John resigned himself to having the two of them along.

In a way he was glad for the company. He was concerned about their welfare, and the worry and upset that Tom and Catherine must be experiencing so he said, "We'll send a message back with one of the scouts at the next station so Tom will know you are with me." Lewis grinned and slipped over to lean against John. Another piece of meat went into the grease pot and the three of them ate their fill.

By the time John cleaned up, he heard Lewis breathing deeply and regularly as he slept. John shook his head and laughed at the persistence of one so young. He was proud of the child. "He's tough enough for this world," he mumbled. John removed a blanket from one of his packs and used it to cover Lewis. Ben opened his eyes the moment John moved and then closed them again when he saw there was no danger.

Snow started falling shortly before dawn and the quietness of winter greeted them when they awoke. It excited Lewis, but John would rather the storm had waited a few days. He told Lewis to fetch some water while he stoked the fire up and started breakfast. John knew that they may have to travel a good distance before they had another warm dry camp so they should start out with a hot meal in their stomachs.

While Lewis was eating, John went outside and located his hobbled horse. It had been foraging on the dried grass and wind-blown corn fodder around the cabin's clearing during the night. He opened a cloth bag and poured out a few handfuls of dried corn for the horse. It would have to carry double now and would need the extra energy. While the horse ate John finished his own meal, then he and Lewis cleaned up and were soon on their way.

As they were leaving the cabin and clearing, Lewis asked John how much further they had to go to reach Mr. Johnson's. John thought a minute and answered, "We're just over a third of the way there. If we don't hit deep snow, we'll be there in a week. We're going to have to take turns walking now and again or we'll wear ol' Stoney out before we go two days in this snow." John reached down and patted his horse on the neck.

John was right about not having a warm dry camp again for awhile. Two nights later they stayed at a small settlement on the west branch of the Susquehanna. It was so new that John did not know it existed until he and Lewis rode into a clearing with fresh chopped tree stumps and smelled the smoke from cook fires. The people there told him they had just come up river that summer before they knew about the war. Now they were hoping to get back to safer territory as soon as the weather broke. They had ranging spies out watching the passes constantly and welcomed this bad weather. They hoped it would keep the Indians at home until spring. John told them that if he could travel in it, the Indians could too.

He left a letter with them for anyone going down stream to Harris' trading post, in hopes it would get to Tom some time during the winter. The residents of the settlement asked John to take along several letters for their families and friends who lived in New York Colony and New England. He would drop them off at William Johnson's.

· · ·

The fourth day after leaving the settlement, John and Lewis came in sight of Fort Johnson. It was the biggest, most beautiful house Lewis had ever seen. It was the first house he ever saw that wasn't a log cabin or a bark hut. An Indian encampment was at a distance behind Mr. Johnson's house.

Lewis was sitting on the bundle of trade goods behind John. Ben was walking along beside the mounted riders, as they rode up to the front entrance of Johnson Hall. John helped Lewis down and was in the process of dismounting himself, when the front door opened and a tall white man dressed in a mixture of Indian and white man's clothing, stepped out the door. He was still buttoning his coat and settling a tri-corn hat on his head as he came out to welcome them.

He walked over to John and Lewis and said, "Welcome strangers. What can I do for you?"

John said, "Sir, my name is John Phares. I'm from down along the Potomac, near Fort Cumberland. Did you receive the letter I sent you two months ago?"

Johnson said, "I did. Come in and warm yourselves, Mr. Phares. We'll talk and see what can be done for your situation."

As they turned to walk toward the house John said, "I would have been here sooner, but I have not been able to travel until last week, and we've been on our way these past ten days."

Mr. Johnson stopped as though he were trying to recall something, and said, "I've heard of you. You've traded down by the forks of the Ohio, haven't you? I've heard you're a fair man to deal with. Weren't you partners with...ahhh Joshua.... Watson? That's it, Joshua Watson."

"He's part of the reason why I'm here, Mr. Johnson. Joshua was going to the fort with my wife when she was took by the Wyandots. It looked like he done his best, they were just too many...he was killed."

Johnson put his left hand on John's shoulders and said, "I'm sorry about Joshua, he was an old friend. I hadn't seen him since...." Trying to recall the last time he saw him, he started to speak again and said, "Well, it's been years . . .funny how that happens... but my people have nothing but good to say about you, and it's good to finally meet you. I'm just sorry it's under these circumstances. Now that you're here, I'll do my best to find something out about your lovely wife."

Taking notice of Lewis and Ben, Johnson asked John who his traveling companions were. John introduced them. Mr. Johnson said, "It looks like the three of you could use a fire to warm the outside of you and hot food to warm your insides. We have both, so…." An Indian youth came out the door at that time and Johnson, changing his train of thought, said, "Here comes Steven. He'll help you with your horse. He turned to Steven and said, "Would you take Mr. Phares' horse round to the barn and make sure it has some feed and water?" Steven nodded his head and held the reins while John unloaded the bundle of trade goods from the horse, then he led Stoney around to the barn and a dry stall. Johnson watched the young man disappear around the corner of the house, then turned his attention back to his guests. He invited them in, saying, "Now, come on in and bring the dog, there's nothing he can hurt here."

John had set the bundle on the steps next to the door. As Johnson passed it, he told John he could leave the bundle inside the hall where there was plenty of room and it would be handy when needed. John put the bundle down inside the entrance way and walked into a large room that had a roaring fire in a large fireplace. Elegant furniture, graced the room; the likes of which John had not seen since leaving Scotland as a lad. Lewis walked with large eyes wandering from the polished floor to the tall ceiling, looking at caved chairs, tables, paintings and other strangely wonderful things.

Johnson invited John to have a seat in one of two matching chairs sitting in front of the fireplace. Lewis and Ben crowded next to each other on the floor at the feet of the adults. In spite of all the costly furniture the fire was most inviting of all. An indentured servant entered the room carrying a tray of food, a pot of tea and a decanter of whiskey. Whiskey was poured for the two men and a cup of tea laced with extra maple sugar, along with a pastry was handed to Lewis. The boy broke off a bite of the pastry and handed it to Ben, who gulped it down and waited for more. Lewis licked at his pastry tasting it thoroughly and slowly then sipped his tea.

The servant, seeing the men filling their pipes took a small tool from above the fireplace and retrieved a live coal from the fire. He carried it to the two men and held it so they could light their pipes. When they had taken several draws on their pipes, and the pleasing smell of fine pipe tobacco had wafted through the room, Johnson said, "Your arrival could not have been timed better. Some Mingos just came in from the Ohio country a few days ago. We'll speak to them; they may know something. You're lucky you're meeting them here instead of out there; the whole area is a mess."

John said, "Yes it is. Worse than I have ever seen it. It seems everything's turned upside down from the southern colonies to the New England colonies, and the border people are caught in the middle."

Johnson saw Steven pass the door and called to him. When the Indian boy came into the room Johnson said, "Steven, would you extend an invitation to the Mingo hunters to meet with us this evening?" Then Johnson got up and went over to a table and picked up a small pouch. He handed it to Steven and told him to give the contents to the hunters as his gift. Steven nodded and said, "Yes, Sir" and left the room to accomplish his errand.

The conversation continued between the two men as they studied one another. They talked about mutual friends, places they had visited, politics, and caught up on the news each had heard. After a while John's eyes would close between sentences as sleep tried to overcome him. This was the most comfortable he had been since leaving Tom's place. The warmth of the fire, and a comfortable chair made him so sleepy he almost shook with the need to sleep.

Seeing this, Johnson told John to just sit and relax in front of the fire because he had some work that needed to be done. He would let John know when news came of the impending meeting. John was asleep before William Johnson finished the invitation. As he moved toward a cherry wood desk Johnson quietly told the servant to get a blanket and cover the sleeping man. Then looking at the floor, he said, "And the lad also" The boy was curled up against the exhausted dog sound asleep.

The sounds of the crackling fire in the fireplace, the ticking of a pendulum clock and occasionally a low snore from one of the sleeping travelers greeted Steven when he returned. Mr. Johnson who was busy at his desk writing a letter. Johnson jumped a little when Steven touched his shoulder and whispered a short message in his ear. He reacted to the message by asking, "A Wyandot?" Steven nodded and said, "Yes, I'm sure" then left the room.

Johnson walked over to John, gently woke him and said, "Steven told me there is a Wyandot with those Mingos, so we may find your wife. He'll be along with the Mingos shortly.' Johnson glanced at the clock and said, "We have time to eat before they arrive. If you come with me, I'll show you where to freshen up, and dinner should be ready by the time we are." John woke Lewis and they followed Johnson to a room at the back of the house where wash basins, warm water and soap were waiting.

Later, after dinner, the men and Lewis returned to the living room where

Steven had lit several candles and laid more coals on the fire. A cold blast of air tried to pull the light from the candle wicks as the sound of the door being opened drew their attention to the hallway. Two Indians wrapped in blankets against the cold were followed by a third Indian. William Johnson stepped forward to greet them. The third Indian stepped out of the shadows and into the lighted room.

It was Yellow-Hand.

Ben growled at him. The young dog had seen and smelled this one before. John said, "Hush, Ben! Lay down!" He had to say it twice and grab Ben and force him to lay next to Lewis. He told Lewis to watch him close. Ben obeyed, Lewis but never took his eyes off of Yellow-Hand. The boy trusted the dog. It made no sense to the child that Ben paid the Mingos men no mind at all but would not take his eyes from the Wyandot. He had never heard Ben so tense. The dog's growls came from so deep within that Lewis felt them as though they screamed, yet they were silent against his ears. Lewis held an arm around Ben's neck. It was plain to Lewis that if he turned Ben loose, he would attack.

They all moved toward the fire and sat down. John produced a tobacco pouch and presented it to the nearest Indian. He filled his pipe and passed it to the next Indian, and so on, until John got the pouch back. Steven got a coal from the fireplace with the little tool he had used earlier, and went to each adult and presented it for them to light their pipes. Steven was familiar with this ceremony. He then left the room to fetch a pot of tea and some food.

Nothing could be rushed; each step of this ceremony must be observed. First the welcome, next the ritual of smoke, then food and drink, then another pipe, and finally they would arrive at the purpose of the meeting.

Time passed. It was all John could do to hold his questions. At last one of the Indians set a delicate tea cup down, now emptied of the tea it had held, and brought out his pipe again. The rest finished their meal and retrieved their pipes. Steven repeated the earlier exercise of getting a coal from the fireplace for them to light their pipes. During the whole time, Lewis had not said a word and his eyes betrayed no emotion as he carefully looked each Indian up and down. Ben had relaxed a little, but each time Yellow Hand moved, Ben raised his head and a low growl rumbled in his chest that Lewis could feel.

After a few puffs, John said, "I am happy to be with you. Mr. Johnson has asked you to be here on my behalf in a matter that is close to my heart. I come bearing many gifts to open your eyes and unplug your ears, and to clear your throats, so that you may speak to me of these things." John paused, then said, "My wife was taken by warriors who have mistaken me for their enemy. I am searching for news of her, that I may find her and bring her back to her lodge. My heart is heavy. I must ask if you, or your Wyandot neighbor, may know of these things. She was taken before the leaves were full, from near the Cohongoronto (Potomac) River as she crossed the Caicutuck (Wills Creek) stream."

John took three strings of wampum out of a pouch and handed one to each of the Indians as part of this ceremony. Then he said, "These words are to tell you what is in my heart. I have many gifts to reward those who have taken care of my wife. Do you have words that may lead me to her?"

Only one of the Indians spoke English so he looked at the other two then started speaking to them in Mingo. The other Mingo shook his head no, then they both looked at Yellow-Hand. He leaned forward and began to speak in Wyandot with hand signs that John knew well. The Mingo who spoke English translated for John. Everyone listened to the words that were spoken and then translated.

"Yellow Hand's words are these: "I have traveled to greet my peaceful brothers. War is heavy in the land. I have always been peaceful. I have not lifted my hand against the white people."

Yellow Hand waited until his words had been translated. The talk of gifts intrigued him. He put on a tender face before he spoke again.

"I have seen the woman you speak of. She was brought into our village before the leaves were full. I was kind to her....but when some white men tried to stop the warriors from taking her, many warriors were killed, and their blood demanded revenge."

Yellow-Hand chanced a look at John as the Mingo translated. John understood his insinuation that it was the fault of the men he led that his wife was put in additional danger, but he did not know it was Yellow Hand that had taken his friend's scalp. He would not give gifts if he knew that, so Yellow hand pretended to have only heard of these things. He would have loved to smile, but it would ruin the cut he planned for this white man's heart. The translator finished to that point and Yellow-Hand continued.

"I have come to join my brothers here because I am peaceful and I love all brothers red and...white. Looking into John's eyes he put on the most tender expression that he was capable of presenting and continued.

"I tried to save your woman, but they burned her and did many bad things to her.... they would not listen to my council."

Yellow-Hand sat back as the speech was being translated. When the words were understood by John and Lewis, Lewis hid his head under the blanket. John was speechless. There was no sound. Even the Mingo knew this was hard news for any man and remained silent.

Thoughts raced through John's mind. To the world he looked composed but hurt. Inside he was a thunderstorm of emotion. This man had tried to help his wife, but he failed. John didn't know whether to hate him or love him. He was numb. John slowly got up and walked to the door and into the hallway. His shoulders slumped. His spirit was broken. The Mingos reached out and patted John as he passed them. Yellow-Hand stood up to watch John. He had cut this man and twisted the knife in him just as surely as if the knife had been real. The devastation caused almost as much pleasure as if the blood he spilled this day was real blood and the pain as deadly. He enjoyed John's misery.

John stepped out into the cold night air and looked up at the stars while the Mingos, who had started to follow him, returned to the fire. In a few minutes, he regained his composure. Love fought with hate but his love for Rachel was stronger. His love for Rachel demanded action and she would no longer be with him to be loved. Aligning his mind and body with his resolve to care for her he knew he would befriend this man who tried to help his wife. The Indian had failed, but that was nothing: John had failed her too.

He walked back inside to where his bundle lay in the hall and pulled out a pouch and his rifle. The gun was in a case made from a piece of blanket. He walked back into the room almost in a trance. John struggled with the buckles on the pouch. He finally got it opened, and handed each of the Mingo Indians a present. Then John picked up the cased rifle and slid it from the covering. The Indians let out a gasp of admiration at the beauty and grace of the rifle. The firelight reflected off the hand-rubbed finish and the beautiful grain of the curly maple wood used in its construction seemed to be floating on glass as it undulated down the length of the rifle.

John walked up to Yellow-Hand. With quiet words and eyes almost brimming with tears he said, "I encourage you to continue to follow the path of peace. You will need a good rifle to provide meat for your family. I thank you for trying to save my wife. I am grateful for your kindness to her. I give this rifle in gratitude for the kindness you showed her."

John then walked over to Lewis and picked him up, blanket and all. He whispered his gratitude to Johnson then turned and carried Lewis out of the house. Ben fell in next to John as they left the room, giving a final audible growl as he passed Yellow-Hand. Yellow-Hand followed them to the door with the rifle in his hands. As John carried Lewis around the corner of the house, Yellow-Hand said in a low voice, "Fool."

CHAPTER TWENTY FOUR

Winter Camp in the Uncharted Wilderness

Rachel placed her knife back into the belt sheath, and stepped back from the birch tree she had been carving. She reached up with her right hand and traced the words she had carved into the smooth surface of the tree. — JOHN—. Tears started down her cheeks and a terrible loneliness engulfed her.

She leaned against the tree while she regained control of her emotions. Snow had started to fall, so she bent down and picked up the bundle of firewood that lay at her feet. She took hold of the burden strap around and swung the bundle from the snow-covered ground onto her shoulders then trudged toward the clearing that held the little bark-covered longhouse. The shelter was nearly engulfed in the drifting snows of winter. Rachel could see the faint flicker of firelight from inside the shelter through the dusk of approaching darkness.

The depth of the snow and the advanced stage of her pregnancy made it hard for Rachel to walk. When she entered the lodge, she was exhausted, but emotionally she felt better after the walk. She was not sure how the carving made her feel. It was something she could touch and feel. Though it brought pain she thought it brought more comfort. It gave her a certain hold on the past in a way that she couldn't even explain to herself.

Rachel put the bundle of firewood down, removed the burden strap and went to a large pouch. Tucking the strap into her pouch she shuffled the contents so she could reach some cloth and a sewing needle. Then she went to the fire and took a seat next to Little Fawn.

Rachel took several stitches on the little shift she was making for her unborn child, then she hesitated as she began watching Little Fawn working quill-work onto a pouch. The tiny little porcupine quills had been dyed with bright colors, and were now being worked into beautiful patterns. Each pattern meant something; possibly telling of a past event, honoring the source of some kind of power or deity, or maybe designate the owner of the article. The velvet softness of the brain-tanned deer hide, had lovingly been cut into a pattern and sewn with the sinew from a deer to form a graceful bag. Little Fawn would have many uses for the bag; maybe it would hold the charms and medicines she used to heal her family, or some tobacco for a ceremony, or it might just be a beautiful useful bag to keep and use, or trade for something that could not be had in the wilderness.

Rachel reached over and touched the finished quill work. Little Fawn looked up and smiled as Rachel pulled back her hand. After a minute or two of watching Little Fawn work, Rachel touched her on the arm and made sewing motions with her hands, and at the same time, in broken English and Wyandot, asked, "Would you show me?" Then she asked again in Wyandot.

Little Fawn erupted with happiness when she realized what Rachel was asking. She babbled in Wyandot and hugged her, then she pulled Rachel over to her and started instructing her in the ancient art of quill working. Little Fawn would interrupt her instructions every once in a while just to smile and hug Rachel. This was a dream come true for Little Fawn. Her daughter, Catches-The-Wind, did not like quill work until this winter. Little Fawn thought she would never be able to pass this knowledge on to anyone in her family, until now.

Jacob had been sitting on the other side of the fire, smoking his pipe and watching. Maybe things weren't going to be as bad as he thought. Here were two spirits becoming as one, a mother and a daughter. He himself had been drawn to this girl. it was good to have Catches the Wind back again. Still he worried about Night-Bird-Singing. She had such a dark look on her face as this bonding between red mother and white daughter became more obvious each day. Somehow she thought the bond was formed because the girl was with child. She would not even acknowledge Rachel's presence, and it had gotten worse as the pregnancy became more visible and the winter wore on.

Jacob finished smoking his pipe as he thought about these things, then cleaned it carefully and replaced it in his pipe bag. In a few moments he laid aside the pouch containing the pipe and tobacco and got up. He glanced at Night-Bird-Singing, and left the lodge with a worried look on his face. It was still snowing and looked like it might continue for some time to come. Jacob saw movement at the edge of the clearing through the falling snow, and became tense until he recognized the approaching figure as the snow-covered Kitcheogeemaw.

Jacob greeted Kitcheogeemaw with, "Ahh.... How went the hunt? We were starting to worry."

Kitcheogeemaw answered, "Badly, three days and I saw no game." Jacob responded with encouragement as he always did, "Tomorrow may be better." Jacob drew back the blanket that covered the lodge doorway so Kitcheogeemaw could enter. He was greeted by a relieved family, happy at the return of their provider. When Kitcheogeemaw had taken a seat near the fire, Strong Woman ladled the last of the food into a wooden bowl and took it to him. He refused it when he saw it was the last of the food. Strong Woman told him they had already eaten and everyone agreed as he looked at them one by one. Only then did Kitcheogeemaw take the food. No one had eaten that day, but all knew that Kitcheogeemaw had not eaten for more than a day and had been out in the cold and snow hunting for food to feed them. They knew he needed strength to go again the next day.

Jacob sat down in his usual place, picked up a small dog and absent mindedly started petting it as Kitcheogeemaw was eating. The rest of the family caught Jacob's attention. Of one accord they seemed to look at the empty pot sitting next to the fire and then at the dog he was petting. Jacob looked down at the dog, then at the empty food pot and up at his hungry family. After thinking about this for a moment, waited until they were otherwise occupied and pushed the dog protectively under the blanket he had around himself, and said, "A little bird told me, the snow will bring better hunting tomorrow."

Little Fawn raised her eyes without raising her head and looked at Jacob as he made the prediction. She knew what a character he was. Then she continued with her instructions to Rachel.

Suddenly Rachel sat up straight. She smiled, and reached over and took Little Fawn's hand and placed it on her stomach. In a moment Little Fawn broke into a grin that lighted her face. She told the rest of the family that the baby had moved against her hand. Everyone clapped and giggled with happiness. Everyone, except Night-Bird-Singing.

Little Fawn said, "This one must be a warrior; he just kicked me again!" Even Kitcheogeemaw broke into a grin as he set the empty bowl down, and reached for, and lit, his pipe.

Rachel had tried to keep track of the months so she would have some idea of when the baby was due, but it was difficult. She thought Christmas must be approaching soon, but the baby would not come for a long time after that. This evening she felt so light-hearted that she started to sing of another Child who had been born in a manger over 1700 years before. The songs were familiar to Jacob, though he had not heard them in many years. He began to sing along with Rachel, and for the rest of the evening, the two of them sang many songs over and over again. The others listened, and as they became familiar they joined in to keep time, hum or sing. Strong-Woman didn't know what she was singing, but by the end of the evening, she could sing some of the old Christmas songs too, part in Wyandot and part in English. Little Fawn asked what the songs meant. With the help of Jacob translating for her, Rachel told the family the story of Christmas in her simple frontier language.

"Long ago the Creator took pity on his children and sent his son to save them from the Evil Spirit. He came into the world in the form of a human baby, and was born to a woman who had never been with a man, so the world would know that He was from the Creator, and that the Creator could do anything. This Child was born to die for those who would believe in Him. He would be a man who would be proof of the Creator's goodwill. He could take every punishment instead of letting his people be punished forever. His perfect blood would cover up the evil deeds of man forever, so they could enter the presence of the Great Spirit when they die. This is the season of the birth of the baby who had done all this, so we sing.

Each of the family members shook their heads in wonder at this story. They had always sacrificed to the evil spirits in hopes that there would be no harm done to them. They did not think it was necessary to sacrifice to the Great Spirit, as he would never do them any harm. It was decided they would have to think on this. It seemed too easy; all they had to do was believe.

The short winter days and long cold nights crept by. There were times of hunger and periods of feast. Kitcheogeemaw had left to go hunting early the morning after they had celebrated Christmas, and as Jacob had predicted, hunting was better. Kitcheogeemaw hunted in a different direction than he normally did, and found a heard of deer that had yarded up as a result of the heavy snowfall. This was not an uncommon habit with deer during bad winters and heavy snow. They would come together in varying numbers and pack the snow down in small areas called yards. As the snow got deeper, the deer could reach higher and higher to branches that have buds on them. These buds were full of strength and animals such as wolves were more reluctant to attack a herd of strong deer that could defend themselves.

Kitcheogeemaw was able to kill several deer with his bow and arrows before they realized they were in danger. That hunt kept the family in meat for nearly a month before he had to hunt full time again. During this time, Kitcheogeemaw was able to concentrate on trapping. It was a good year and many beaver, mink, otter and other fur-bearing animals fell to Kitcheogeemaw's skill. The family would have a good year. He would get many things from the traders when they returned to the summer village.

The weather became so cold after he found the deer yard, that the trees, even in the day time, would burst with a sound so loud it was as though a gun was being fired. During this cold spell, Kitcheogeemaw could not stay out overnight as he normally did when he combined hunting with trapping. For weeks he had to return to the lodge each evening. The young women and children spent most of the time during the short winter days gathering firewood. They had to travel farther and farther away from camp to find dead trees that would burn. When they dragged the limbs of trees and dead saplings back to camp, the wood had to be placed next to the fire to thaw before it would burn well. Ice from the frozen stream was placed in a pot and melted over the fire for drinking water. Even water that was dipped through the ice covered stream froze before they could carry it back to the lodge. Anything that was more than a few feet from the fire froze within minutes.

The outside of the lodge looked like a pile of dirty snow until the next storm, but when it snowed Rachel thought it looked as though a new coat of white paint had been applied. Then the smoke from the cook fire discolored it again. At first the winter seemed pleasant to Rachel. As time went on it seemed like winter would never end.

One morning when the fire was being built up for cooking, the sound of a drop of water hitting a hot surface was heard. It hit the cooking pot with a sizzling sound, then another and another followed. It was not the heat of the fire that was melting the ice around the smoke hole, but warm air, and it was the first hint of spring; it was wonderful. There would still be cold days and nights, but the promise of spring was here. The family, for the first time in many weeks, did not feel the blast of bitter cold air when the blanket was drawn back as Kitcheogeemaw stepped out to greet the morning sun. Sugar-making time would soon arrive and there was much to be done.

They could not put away their snow shoes yet. That night, the temperature took a nose dive and a blizzard blew in from the northwest. It seemed as though winter was clinging to the land and refusing to admit the sun was becoming victorious over the darkness of long nights. It was many days before the promised spring arrived for good.

When it finally did arrive, Strong-Woman was in charge of gathering the maple sap. She and Night-Bird-Singing were very busy making new buckets and repairing old ones. They made them from the bark of the birch tree. It took several days to have enough ready. By the time they were finished, the buds on the trees were swelling, the sap was rising and the snow melting in the warming sun of early spring.

After months of snow and bitter cold, it felt good to see bare ground appearing here and there. The area around the camp turned into a quagmire of mud and water from the melting snow. If the lodge had not been built on a slight rise of ground, it would have been flooded from quick spring thaws. The lodge was full of wet moccasins hanging up to dry.

The fur-bearing animals were past their prime and shedding their winter coats, so Crane and Kitcheogeemaw were busy gathering and oiling his few metal traps, scraping the hides that still needed work, and preparing them for transport to the traders. Wooden traps had to be dismantled so no animal would be trapped to suffer needlessly after he no longer made his rounds. The trap line extended many miles and kept Kitcheogeemaw away from camp for long periods of time. He hunted as he gathered the metal traps and so at times, he had to make several trips back and forth to camp from many miles away, carrying meat for the family.

Strong-Woman could not help, as she was busy with the maple sugar making. Crane was kept busy in camp tanning the hides and bundling the furs into packs for transport. He had tended the traps near camp during the winter. He could not travel great distances any more, but he was expert at the things he could still do and this made things easier for Kitcheogeemaw.

Much firewood had to be gathered, not only for the cooking fire, but to keep a fire under the big iron kettle they used to boil the sap into syrup and finally sugar. Rachel was determined to help as much as she could. She carried two large bark buckets to each maple tree, and poured the sap from the smaller buckets, which had been catching the sap from each tree, into the ones she was carrying. She walked up to a maple tree near the birch tree where she had carved

—I LOVE JOHN—

In the warming air it seemed so long ago. During the past weeks, she had visited this place less and less often. She poured more sap into her buckets, stopped to cradle her belly for a moment. The work did not seem to hurt her, but she had felt something different as she poured. As she picked up the larger buckets she glanced up at the weathered carving and then at the faraway wigwam that was only a tiny gleam of reflected light through the still bare woods. She seemed to feel less emptiness in her heart now. "Affection" was the only word that could be used to describe the feelings she had toward the family in the little clearing. She turned and walked toward the wigwam.

Night-Bird-Singing and the children were tending the fire when Rachel carried the buckets of sap into camp. Night-Bird-Singing gave Rachel a cold look and did not offer to help as she sat one bucket down and poured the other into the iron kettle. The steam rose as the cool sap mixed with the frothy boiling sap. Rachel set the empty bucket down and reached for the full one when she felt her first clear labor pain. She grabbed her stomach with both hands.

This caught the attention of Little Fawn and she went to her. In Wyandot, Little Fawn said, "It is time." As Little Fawn led Rachel toward the little birthing shelter they had built several days before, she told Night-Bird-Singing to be sure she stayed with the fire and tended the pot of sap. Then Little Fawn yelled to Strong-Woman and told her that it was time and that Catches-The-Wind was in labor and to come help her.

Strong-Woman came out of the lodge carrying a pouch and rushed to the birthing shelter. Night-Bird-Singing stared after Rachel and Little Fawn as they disappeared into the shelter, and then went back to tending the boiling sap. She yelled at one of the children who quickly put more firewood under the pot and stepped out of her reach. The other children scattered in search of more wood. Night-Bird-Singing angrily poured the remaining bucket of sap into the pot and began vigorously stirring its boiling contents.

Throughout the afternoon, she tried to ignore the activity in the birthing shelter, but she could not keep her attention from it. At the front of the shelter, a small campfire had been started and a pot of water was placed over it. The contents had been replenished several times as the water boiled away, but water was always waiting to rinse the soiled rags they used to keep Rachel clean. Low moans could be heard, as well as the voices of Little Fawn and Strong-Woman. Once in a while one of them would dash from the shelter to the lodge for something and then return to apply herbs or refill the pot with water. The sun hung high in the sky and then dipped toward the horizon as time wore on. The children returned again and again with wood. The tree sap became thick and turned to syrup and Night-Bird-Singing continued to tend the pot. But her mind was on what was happening in that little shelter.

Inside the shelter, Rachel was trying not to cry out from the agony. Little Fawn wiped the sweat from Rachel's face as Strong-Woman asked, "Why you not cry out?" Between contractions, Rachel, through clinched teeth, said, "I am as strong as Indian women…."

Strong-Woman translated this into Wyandot and both older women laughed. Little Fawn said something to Strong-Woman that Rachel couldn't understand, and they both laughed again. Strong-Woman then in broken English said, "Catches-The-Wind, you should not believe everything men tell you… You scream if you want to!" She handed Rachel a piece of wet cloth to chew on. Moments later Night-Bird-Singing and Jacob were both startled by the sudden sound of a lusty scream that came from the birthing shelter. After a while the screaming stopped and was replaced by the cry of a little baby.

Night-Bird-Singing ceased her activity and looked toward the birthing shelter, with a longing that only a woman who cannot give birth could understand.

Kitcheogeemaw returned to camp well after dark and saw Jacob dancing outside the lodge beside the fire where the maple sap pot had been. Kitcheogeemaw was a little concerned: It wasn't that the old man couldn't move quickly or well if he wanted to, but Jacob hadn't done such things for a long, long time. Kitcheogeemaw knew there were no special days or events to celebrate, so he wondered if Jacob had been touched by the Great Spirit while he was away, or had found something to smoke or drink that would affect him in this manner. He approached Jacob with curiosity and asked, "What is this ceremony?

Jacob grinned, "This is no ceremony. The baby is here! He will be a great hunter!"

A baby's cry was heard coming from the shelter and Kitcheogeemaw squatted down right where he had been standing to contemplate this event. Jacob returned to his dance and sang until the sounds echoed through the woods around him. Little Fawn had made Night-Bird-Singing sit at the entrance of the birthing shelter to keep an eye on Rachel so she and Strong-Woman could rest for a few moments. Night-Bird-Singing sullenly refused to watch Rachel tend to the baby, but kept her attention on the fire. She saw Kitcheogeemaw looking at her from where Jacob was dancing.

Night-Bird-Singing reached for another piece of wood and placed it on the fire as Rachel held her baby and started to hum an old English lullaby. In a few minutes, Rachel's attention was drawn to Night-Bird-Singing. She noticed the young woman had not looked at the baby. Rachel stopped humming the lullaby and in Wyandot said, "Night-Bird-Singing...?" Night-Bird-Singing would not move or acknowledge Rachel for several moments, then she sneaked a peek inside the shelter. Her inexpressive face was lit by the fire burning next to her. Rachel said in Wyandot, "Please come here."

Night-Bird-Singing hesitated, then quietly entered the shelter and sat next to Rachel. Rachel pulled a fur mantle from the baby's face to show Night-Bird-Singing, who looked at the finely sculpted little face but refused to satisfy her desire to touch. Rachel sensed the other woman's struggle, but she also sensed a softness that took hold of Night-Bird-Singing's heart as she looked at the little eyes, nose, and lips. Night-Bird-Singing was captivated by the infant.

Rachel was no longer afraid of this girl. The softness made her love her. She had grown to know it was pain and not hatred that made Night-Bird-Singing avoid her all this time. Rachel tiredly reached out and took hold of Night-Bird-Singing's arm and pulled her closer. Weakly she placed the baby in Night-Bird-Singing's arms. In Wyandot, Rachel said, "I am tired, please watch him while I rest. Before she let go, Rachel looked intently at the young girl whose heart had just been captured. She watched the girl's eyes explore the way the fur of the protective mantle blended with the infant's own softness. Rachel said softly, "I know that among my new people you too are his mother."

Night-Bird-Singing blinked and reluctantly pulled her eyes from the baby to look into Rachel's eyes. She needed to measure the sincerity of the words. Her eyebrows raised in question? "I am mother?"

She inhaled a breath that quivered and held it while she reached out, at last, to touch the cheek of the child still held by both women. Slowly she reached until she saw her finger touching the infant, but the skin was so soft she could not feel it on her fingertip. So soft. The infant opened its eyes as Rachel let go and Night-Bird-Singing took a moment to adjust the baby in her arms. A drop of water splashed against the infant cheek, surprising Night-Bird Singing. She did not know where the water came from. Then she realized the water had come from her own eyes. Another tear glistened on her dark, winter-brown skin as she wiped the little cheek dry again and whispered, "I am mother". All her breaths quivered as she moved to gently hug the baby to her. With tear whetted lips she kissed a tiny hand.

Rachel watched Night-Bird-Singing gently rocking the baby with closed eyes. As another tear ran down Night-Bird-Singing's cheek, Rachel reached out and brushed it away. She noticed Little Fawn was back, but had stayed outside to look in at the moment she had long been hoping for: Catches-The-Wind and Night-Bird-Singing were truly sisters once again. The fatigue of childbirth swept over Rachel. Her baby was warm and safe in the arms of Night-Bird-Singing and guarded tirelessly by a loving grandmother. She closed her eyes in sleep.

CHAPTER TWENTY FIVE

Weeks Later – Exterior of Lodge

The camp was full of peace and tranquility. Insects were buzzing and the songs of birds were heard from every quarter as they arrived in increasing numbers each day. Kitcheogeemaw had fallen asleep in the warm afternoon sun with his pipe still smoking at his side. He was at peace with the world. Rachel was nursing baby Jonathan amid stretched beaver skins and dressed deer hides. Strong-Woman was hauling some basswood bark into camp. She and Night-Bird-Singing were making ropes to secure their winter catch of furs for transport to the traders. The bark had soaked until it smelled like excrement, then it was cleaned, pulled apart, and twisted into ropes that would be strong when dry and even stronger when wet. Crane was busy wiping bear grease on the steel traps against rust and securing them for the summer while they were away.

Jacob had walked into the woods with his walking stick and a leather bag across his shoulders. Baggage was sitting everywhere in preparation for the journey to the summer village and their old friends. Kitcheogeemaw opened his eyes at the honking of north-bound geese. He watched them for a minute or two, then closed his eyes again, hoping no one had noticed he was awake. But Rachel had seen him watching the geese. She looked up and followed their flight, and when she looked back down at Kitcheogeemaw he had already closed his eyes again, but she knew he wasn't asleep.

The baby had finished nursing and wanted to play, so Rachel walked over to Kitcheogeemaw and gently kicked his arm to get his attention before she placed the baby on his stomach. The sound of cooing and giggling from the little fellow delighted Kitcheogeemaw and he opened his eyes again and held the child up at arm's length. The baby slobbered in his face. Kitcheogeemaw grimaced and then laughed, and the baby started laughing. Night-Bird-Singing went to them and fussed at him for being rough. She walked over and took the baby out of his hands, and started cooing to it. A look of disappointment came over Kitcheogeemaw's face, he had been enjoying the baby.

Rachel smiled with contentment. Her greatest fear had been defeated by the affection everyone was lavishing on her son. She picked up a burden strap and walked into the woods to pick up plentiful firewood that had been revealed by the melted snow. Not far away her weathered carving caught her attention.

—I LOVE JOHN—

was now deep brown against the pale bark. She wandered slowly to the tree, picking up firewood as she moved, then stopped at the tree to touch it one more time. She put down the firewood she had gathered and reached up to trace the carving with her finger. Her words came as though John was standing within reach.

"John…I wish you could see him…he's beautiful…we have to go soon…I miss you, but it's not so bad…. I…."

She was silenced as a voice startled her. "Catches-The-Wind!"

She spun around and saw Jacob sitting beneath a nearby tree, holding a book he had been reading. Rachel asked, "What are you doing here?"

Jacob answered by asking, "What are you doing here?"

Rachel was embarrassed by what Jacob may have seen and heard so she tried to change the subject as she walked over to him. She asked, "Are you reading?"

Jacob looked down at the book and answered, "Well…. yes."

Rachel said, "It seems odd to see an Indian reading."

"Not as odd as naming a tree John."

Embarrassed, but still trying to take attention away from what she had been doing, she asked, "What are you reading?"

Jacob held his hand up for Rachel to assist him in standing. When she had helped him get to his feet, he handed her the book. It was a Bible. Wrinkling his brow as though he were confused, he pointed to it and said, "I have read that book many times…it has taught me different things than it taught my teacher…maybe his book was different…." Jacob stretched his back and straightened himself as though to dismiss the subject.

Rachel returned his Bible then stepped over to where she had left the firewood, but she was not ready to end this conversation. The old man had avoided and parried her questions about his past all winter. She was not going to let him wiggle out of this conversation. She had grown to care about the old Indian and she wanted to know the man who so obviously had grown to love her. She tied the burden strap around the wood and picked it up, then with resolve strengthening her voice said, "Jacob, when you talked some time ago about how we all have our own wounds, I could see you have a slow healing one...what is your wound?"

Jacob put the Bible back into the leather pouch, walked over to where she was standing and looked into her eyes. In a very quiet voice he told her, "As a young boy, I was educated by the English because my father wanted me to know the writing as the English do. My father thought I could protect our people in trading. When I grew older, I returned to my sister's longhouse. Here, I have a resting place, but I have no home. I am different because of what I have learned. I learned of continents, science, math and other civilizations. History made me see that our people will not be able to live forever, as we do now. Some wounds can be felt long before they are inflicted. I fear, someday, my people will be like me.... perhaps they may not even have a resting place...this is the wound I feel."

When Jacob finished speaking he held his arm out to her. She adjusted her bundle and put her hand in the crook of his arm. They turned and together stepped through the forest toward the distant clearing that contained the fragile bark lodge. Rachael could suddenly and clearly see what Jacob was talking about. In one or two seasons the camp would disappear into the ground without a trace. Rachael knew very well the feeling of rest while still not feeling at home. Through the trees they could see movement that both knew was Little Fawn building up the cook fire with wet wood. Smoke could be seen curling above the wigwam. Jacob said, "She is wanting the firewood, we must go."

As they walked back to camp arm in arm she lay her head against his shoulder in the filtered light that had been stained green by reflections from the leaves. For a quick instant, Jacob understood what people must mean when they spoke of home. Home was where people rested together. But it would not last. Tomorrow at this time, they would be many miles away from the lodge and Rachel's tree.

CHAPTER TWENTY SIX

The Summer Village

Kitcheogeemaw's eyes were focused on the distant shore as he paddled the dugout through the calm water, Crane followed behind him in the bark canoe. Both vessels were packed with the family belongings of Little Fawn and Strong-Woman. Winter camp was behind them for another year and the summer village was just ahead. Their hearts were light as they looked forward to seeing friends and trading their furs for the household goods they needed.

Friends greeted them as they pulled into shore, happy to see one another again. Kitcheogeemaw admired a horse being led by one of his friends. "Wait," he said, and walked toward Rachel and her baby. Kitcheogeemaw took the baby from Rachel so he could show off his new family member. Rachel trusted Kitcheogeemaw with her son. She watched them go then turned to help the other women carry furs to the trader's camp. Suddenly she saw the one person she hoped would not be there at the summer camp – Yellow-Hand!

He was standing with some other warriors. He saw Rachel and gave her the same evil look she had seen so many times before. She turned her head away and stayed close to the other women. Kitcheogeemaw mounted his friend's horse to give the baby a ride. He called to Rachel, "Catches-the-Wind." She waved and smiled. She was glad the child was with Kitcheogeemaw. Then she turned her attention once again to the bundles of goods. The sight of Yellow Hand had disturbed her. Her mind returned to John, and she felt the pain of separation grab her heart once more.

That evening Rachel was inside the longhouse as Strong-Woman came in and put down a bundle of goods she had gotten in trade. Strong-Woman spoke in broken English, "That all."

Rachel was puzzled. "You traded all the furs for one bundle of goods?" she asked.

Strong-Woman replied, "All gone. Much whiskey."

"But we had nine bundles of furs," said Rachel. "Two would have bought these goods. All the rest went for whiskey?"

Strong-Woman did not understand all that Rachel had said, but she got the drift and said, "All whiskey. No more bundle. All whiskey."

Rachel noticed suddenly that it was late in the day. She peered out the door of the longhouse, wondering where Kitcheogeemaw had gone with the baby. She had spent several hours together with Night-Bird-Singing as she took the baby to show him off to her friends. She had nursed him until he slept and when he woke Kitcheogeemaw took him. The baby was always happy when he was fresh from a nap. Kitchogeemaw was always careful. He was proud of how big the child had grown. But now wanted him in her arms again.

She could see campfires with men sitting around them already getting drunk from the whiskey. There was a lot of noise in the village. Rachel became frightened. A fight broke out and sparks from a fire sparkled in the air as someone tripped into the flames. She turned to Night-Bird-Singing and asked where Kitcheogeemaw was. She didn't know. Together the concerned women left the longhouse to find him.

The two women moved through the village. Rachel was nearly frantic until she saw Kitcheogeemaw and Jacob lifting the child up into the air to show another warrior the child's long legs. "Thank, God," she whispered, and began to relax. Kitcheogeemaw saw Rachel and smiled as he greeted her and Night-Bird-Singing. Rachel returned his smile. When Jacob saw the two women, he took the baby from Kitcheogeemaw and handed him to his mother.

"You go home," he told them as he walked away with them. "The baby is fine here even with whiskey, but the whiskey might make some of the warriors see a white woman and not Catches-the-Wind. Now go home and stay there." Jacob returned to the campfire

Night-Bird-Singing and Rachel continued walking back through the village toward their longhouse. They carefully avoided two French Traders and several drunken Indians. As they shifted between two lodges Night-Bird Singing collided with another man causing his kettle of whiskey to spill. He was already angry when he turned toward them. It was Yellow-Hand.

Yellow-Hand was drunk. And he was angry. He shoved Rachel back even though he could see she was carrying a baby, but Yellow-Hand didn't care about the baby. He looked stupidly at her, his thoughts mired in whiskey. At last he recognized her. He laughed. He had been planning this meeting for a long time, but the whiskey made him forget half the speech he had prepared. With a grin on his face, he showed Rachel the rifle that John had given him. He had been taking it with him all day as he bragged about the deception of John Phares. But he did not tell Rachel he had deceived John to get this gun. He told her he had killed the man who owned this gun.

He told her, "This winter I hunted your husband's scalp. When I killed him, I took this also."

Night-Bird-Singing, using broken English and hand signals, told Rachel, "He lies. NO scalp!"

Rachel wanted to get away from Yellow-Hand. The women turned to go. Yellow-Hand was enraged because his torment had been deflected by Night-Bird-Singing. With a wild swing he hit Rachel in the back with the butt of the rifle, slamming her into the ground with the baby still in her arms. Looking up she saw Night-Bird-Singing pulling her arm but she could not hear her words. She seemed to be screaming, but there was no sound. A few heads loomed over her as people pulled her gently to her side. Everything was quiet. Then as her hearing started to return she heard Night-Bird-Singing crying shrilly. She felt pain, but was still numb. Then she noticed that there was no sound coming from the baby. Yellow-Hand staggered away.

Rachel couldn't seem to speak or move, but she saw Night-Bird-Singing pick up the infant and run toward her family's lodge, leaving Rachel on her hands and knees on the ground.

By the time Night-Bird-Singing walked into the lodge her face was wet with tears and she was crying softly. She could say nothing to Little Fawn or Strong-Woman when she entered the lodge. Her breath seemed to choke her when she tried to form words. She could only sit down on her sleeping mat, holding the baby to her bosom, and rocking back and forth. Little Fawn gently brushed her daughter's hair away from her tears and then pulled back the blanket from the baby's face, and she knew there was nothing to be done for him.

Just then Rachel staggered into the lodge, still disoriented from the blow she received. She moved slowly to where Night-Bird-Singing had the attention of the women.

Little Fawn turned to Rachel and said, "He is no more!"

Suddenly Little Fawn seemed to become an old woman. She got up and walked out of the lodge crying loudly, "He is no more! Her voice broke again and again, but she continued crying in the deepening darkness, "He is no more!" She repeated the words over and over as she wandered almost aimlessly through the village. Others heard her words and they started crying the same message. Shrill crying rippled through the village.

When Kitcheogeemaw heard Little Fawn's cry, he ran to the lodge and saw the lifeless baby, still in the arms of Night-Bird-Singing. Rachel lay with her face touching the the pale cheek of the baby. He stood powerless. Dust settled. Stew burned in the kettle. dogs tucked their tails and moved outside or to the corners of the lodge. Weeping melded until it became impossible to determine who made any particular sound. Then silently turning and leaving, he went to the fire pit, took ashes and charcoal in his hands and blackened his face. He began to sing.

When Little Fawn returned Night-Bird-Singing gave the child to her mother and put her arm around Rachel. Rachel reached out to Night-Bird-Singing and Little Fawn so they would not go away with her little boy. They knelled there in the dirt for a long time, clinging to each other. Weeping.

CHAPTER TWENTY SEVEN

Five Days Later at the Graveside

Five days later the morning sun rose higher in the sky, but darkness filled Rachel's heart. Her face was streaked with dirt, grime, and charcoal furrowed with tear stains. Covered in a dirty blanket, she sat in front of the remains of a small fire, staring at the grave with blank grief-stricken eyes. She was as still as a statue. A breeze moved her clothing, but she barely even blinked.

First she had lost John, now her son. She was so deep within the blackness of herself she did not hear the approach of Jacob as he came up and sat down next to her. He gently pulled the blanket closer around her shoulders.

"You need to go back to the lodge so you can rest and eat," he told her.

She mumbled, "Why don't they punish Yellow-Hand?"

"The people do not hold him responsible. He was bewitched by the whiskey."

"He killed my baby! Rachel finally moved to look Jacob in the eye.

Jacob looked at the little grave and then back at Rachel. "It is Kitcheogeemaw's responsibility as head of the family to enforce justice. If he were to kill Yellow-Hand now, he would be subject to tribal justice for murder. The people blame our sorrow on the evil spirit in the whiskey."

Rachel said, "The evil spirit is in Yellow-Hand. He has hated me from the very first."

Jacob agreed. "There is much truth in what you say. Yellow-Hand is despised by many people because of his evil ways. He does many things that are harmful to our people. But he cannot be punished for what the whiskey made him do."

Jacob had been holding a bowl of food. He put it in Rachel's hand and said, "Eat!" He stood and walked away.

Rachel called after him. "I blame Yellow-Hand."

Jacob said nothing. He paused to look sadly at Rachel; then turned and walked back to the village.

That afternoon when Rachel went back to the village, she saw Yellow-Hand smoking with two friends. She was stunned when she saw him. She became almost sick, but then she felt a strange strength rising in her stomach. Her fists clinched until her fingernails cut her palms then walked to the lodge. There she saw the other women still dressed in filthy clothes just as she was. Their hair was jagged with large hanks of their black hair missing. They had cut their hair and scratched their skin until it bled. They were still visibly relieved to see Rachel and Little Fawn hurried to give her a bowl of food. Rachel made an effort to eat, but as she did, her eyes caught on a long knife hanging on the wall in a sheath. Her fists clinched tight again.

Rachel waited until everyone in the lodge was asleep. Quietly she got up, took the knife from its sheath and went out into the dark night. First she went to the grave. The bowl of food was empty. Even in the moonlight she could see where dogs had crowded onto the mound of dirt to get to the food. Tears came unbidden to her eyes. She would have never believed anyone could cry so much and still have tears left to cry.

She sat down in the moonlight and tried to remember Bible verses about King David when he fought his enemy. She couldn't. So she picked up the knife and moved silently to the village through the wood smoke that refused to rise. She would find Yellow Hand.

As she neared Yellow-Hand's lodge she became more careful. Men lay exposed to the night on blankets outside their longhouses. Rachel became aware of them more by the snoring and loud breathing than by sight. She looked carefully at each man before moving on to the next. Occasionally a dog would growl, but she smelled like the village so they just let her pass without alarm. In the shadows of the long house she stepped on someone lying on the ground. The smell of whiskey was strong and the man didn't move. She leaned down to identify the drunk. It was Yellow-Hand.

She began to shake. Her heart pounded. Taking the knife in both hands she raised it above her head. Her breath stopped. she wanted to breathe by her lungs would not work. Lowering her arms in hopes of breathing once more she noticed a rifle at his side.

It was the gun Yellow Hand said he had taken from John.

She made up her mind the instant she saw the gun that Yellow Hand could not have it. He'd taken Joshua from them. He may have killed her

151

husband too. He had taken her son from her, but he would not have John's gun. She would burn it before she would let him keep it. She might not have the heart to kill this man no matter how justified she believed such a death would be, but she had plenty of heart to deprive him of the gun her husband made.

She had seen it the night her baby was killed. She knew its form. This rifle was the reason she thought Yellow Hand may have killed her husband: If John was not dead, where did this man get this gun?

No, he would not have it. Laying the knife aside she touched the rifle, feeling for familiar carving made by her husband's hands. The moment she touched it a dog growled from the darkness. Even hidden from the moonlight in the shadow of the longhouse she could see Yellow Hand's eyes blink open. His hand reached her throat and his fingers clamped down hard. She raised the gun and slammed it down across those awful eyes. Then again. And again.

Rachel looked down on his body. His arms quivered powerlessly then stopped. The movements reminded her of the stiffening shakes of a slaughtered hog. She was sure he was dead. With the rifle in one hand she stopped long enough to feel the ground for the pouch and horn. Scooping them she hurried back to her own lodge...

Her own lodge...her own lodge...

She had not been here a full year and so many things had become her own. How had that happened? Jacob. Little Fawn. Strong Woman. Night-Bird-Singing...Kitcheogeemaw...

They were her own.

Could they protect her now? She had killed a man. It is true that she wanted to, but it is also true that she did not want to kill. Her own body stopped her when she had the knife; maybe God had held her breath so she could not cut him like she planned. But when the man began to choke her she resisted and he died.

But no one would believe that.

They would think she carried out the murder that the hate in her heart encouraged. No one would believe that mercy was real enough to stop her breath; real enough to stop the murder. Especially now that he was dead. She slowed her walk and made her feet touch gently on the ground so they would not make much noise.

Could Kitcheogeemaw save her now? People would call for her death.

She would die. No one could stop that from happening. It was just. It was right. Rachel had lived her life in a world where violence waited outside the door of every poor log cabin. Death waited at birth and in old age. But death never had power in her own heart and mind until tonight.

Her legs shook and gave way. She knelled in weakness and thought she could not hold her bowels from soiling where she knelt. She was a murderer. Others killed in self-defense but she was like the man she hated: she had killed for the satisfaction that she thought death would bring. She was a murderer.

Would this stain of hatred taint her for eternity? Would it stain the lives of people she had grown to love? Little Fawn? Night-Bird-Singing? Kitcheogeemaw? . . . Jacob?

No. She would not let it. They would not be associated with her murder. She would go far away from them and they would not have to defend her, lose their friends and be made to be enemies to the people who cried for justice. She would go.

John...she would go back to John.

Back to John...if he was still alive...back to the way things were before she had been taken captive. Maybe God would forgive her. Maybe the people far away would never need to know about the murder she discovered in her heart when he baby died. Home. She would go home where death had always happened but where death had never reigned in her heart.

She gained her feet and let the sick feeling in her bowels pass, then she quickly moved to leave this place while the nighttime hid her.

Leaving the rifle, bag and horn outside the lodge, she went inside and moved past the sleeping forms of her adopted family. Rachel leaned over the sleeping Jacob to reach a pouch containing food, then she picked up her blanket and left the lodge. She did not see Jacob open his eyes and watch her leave.

Rachel knew she must hurry now. She went swiftly to the river bank and chose a bark canoe. She got in and pushed off and paddled downstream. She looked back. Then she turned away. The weakness that made her sick was gone. The canoe moved lightly into deeper water. The air became less smokey and the village soon lay far behind her. She only had half of an unmapped continent between her and the only man who could make her feel clean again.

• • •

Yellow-Hand lay on the ground unconscious, but not dead. A corner of his blanket covered his head. In the morning his wife stepped out of their lodge and saw him with the whiskey kettle spilled on its side. She only looked at him with disgust and walked off.

When she returned to her lodge later, she saw her husband still lying on the ground. She bent over him and gave him a shake which caused the corner of the blanket to fall away from his battered face. She then saw blood and heard Yellow-Hand groan. She was still not overly concerned as she cried out, "Someone come help me." He had made someone mad. It had happened before.

. . .

By mid-morning the following day, Rachel was miles downstream from the summer village. After paddling a few more hours, she pulled the canoe off into the forest so she could get some sleep. She would travel only at night in this land that was so thick with Indian villages. Wrapped in her one blanket, she took a few mouthfuls of the food in her bag. She tried to sleep but it was not easy in the brilliant light of day.

She was on the water again as soon as dusk had deepened into darkness. She hugged the shore where shadows had been cast by starlight and after making sure she was heading at least a little bit East, she continued downstream. She paddled all night until her arms felt like they would break. She constantly watched along the shore line for campfires. At dawn, she found another hiding place in the forest. After taking time to hide the canoe she spread her blanket and holding John's gun in her arms, turned to look at the first rays of the sun. She set the rifle down with the barrel pointed at the rising sun. "East", she whispered. East is where she would find John if he still lived. East was where she would lay her bones beside his if he was dead. She kept her eyes turned in that direction as she wrapped her blanket around her and slept sitting next to her pack.

Rachel traveled East until complete darkness and made a cold camp, but was up as dawn was breaking. She would travel by day and by land now; the water was moving too fast and far the wrong way. She checked for the first time to see if the gun was loaded. It wasn't. First she wiped the gun clean and dry and ran a dry patch down the barrel. Any dampness would wet the powder, so she made very sure the gun was dry. She had watched John load a gun a hundred times so she reached for the pouch and found the measure. Pulling the plug from the powder horn with her teeth like John, she poured the hollowed antler measure full. It seemed the powder was so light it would get lost before it hit the bottom of the barrel, but she knew it would all be gathered up and compacted by the patch of cloth and round ball that she would push down next. Positioning the round ball carefully in the center of a little patch of tightly woven cloth she tried to push it down the bore. It was stuck against the opening; jammed by the tight patch. She grabber a stick and resting it atop the round ball, slapped it with her hand until the ball forced the path into the opening. Now that the ball and patch had been pressed into the opening it was easy to slide the load to the breech using the long slender wooded ramrod. Then she cleaned the lock and primed the pan that held a little powder that the sparks would set on fire. She made sure the frizzen sealed the powder against the touch hole where the flame would pass into the main charge. Fastening her blanket to her pack, she slung the burden strap against her forehead and leaned into the load like she had been taught in the winter camp. She looked exactly like an Indian woman. Picking up John's rifle she, took a little food in her mouth, and started walking East, toward John.

In a few miles Rachel came to a stream. She stopped to get a drink, then waded across and up the bank. A noise behind her and off to the side caught her attention. She stepped quickly behind a tree. She watched a bear came into sight, sniff the air, then amble away. Rachel breathed a sigh of relief and started on her way again.

She walked the rest of the day through the wild forest and dropped wearily to sleep as darkness came. The next day was the same. The rifle and pack had become so heavy her arms and back ached. But she traveled on, heading east toward John.

•   •   •

Yellow-Hand carefully studied the shoreline as his canoe moved through the water. He was watching for any sign of Rachel. He knew her trail would lead back to her home. The pain in his head was still strong. The white woman would pay for what she had done. This time he would find her and do with her as he wanted. There would be no Kitcheogeemaw to protect her. She belonged to Yellow-Hand.

CHAPTER TWENTY EIGHT

The Long Walk

Rachel's food was gone. She had not eaten for a day when she came upon a flock of turkeys. A storm was coming and already she could hear thunder. Rachel noticed that every time it thundered, the turkeys would call out, gobbling loudly. She doubted anyone could hear them over the noise of the thunder they were responding to. Several steps later she stopped. She thought if she could shoot a turkey during the thunder, no one could hear the shot. She was so hungry. Her weakness was slowing her down. She counted the seconds between the claps of thunder. There seemed to be no timing that would work. She listened for the sounds just before the thunder. There were none that would help her. Then she thought to count the time between the lightning and the arrival of the thunder. It was worth a try. Spending precious minutes finding the turkeys she moved carefully within range, then she aimed the rifle at one of the turkeys and counted again. When the thunder was at its loudest she fired. The rain started to fall in earnest just as she bent to pick up the turkey.

She found a broken tree half fallen down and crawled beneath the overhang it formed among the tree branches. Rain ran in rivulet on either side of her as she pulled the feathers off the turkey. She was able to build a fire from debris that had been sheltered by the tree. A short time later the turkey roasted on the flames. While she waited impatiently for it to be done enough to eat she pulled John's gun near the fire so it could dry. She wondered how many more miles she must go. But it didn't matter. She would go east. Always east. It didn't matter how far.

· · ·

At the Wyandot village, Night-Bird-Singing ran into the lodge and told Kitcheogeemaw, Yellow-Hand was hunting Catches-the-Wind. She told him he was gone already for two days now. Kitcheogeemaw knew she had struck Yellow Hand and he was sure to retaliate. He did not blame her for running away. Still, he could not sit here and let Yellow Hand harm his sister. He stood up and asked Strong-Woman to pack food for his travels. Jacob was sitting in the lodge smoking. He was very sad. He put down his pipe and said, "I am going with you, Kitcheogeemaw."

"I must travel quickly," said Kitcheogeemaw. "Many winters ago I would have welcomed you, but not this time."

Knowing the young man was right he hung his head. As Kitcheogeemaw began to put together things he would need Jacob sat down. Then, with a sense of urgency the old man rose again went digging through his things. He found the little book that Sutton had given him. Kitcheogeemaw thought Jacob looked much like a conjurer as he opened a little bottle of black liquid and took out tools to write. The ritual did not take long and Jacob soon blew his breath upon the ink to dry it. The younger man knew the importance of breath, so he knew the marks Jacob put in the little book must carry Jacob with them, just like a pipe and smoke. Folding the little Bible closed again, he bound it tight in its leather pouch. Without a smile he gave it Kitcheogeemaw, and asked him to give it to the girl. He sat back down and stared into the fire wondering where his home was now . . .

. . .

It was still raining the next day. Rachel gathered up her things, wrapped the rifle in her blanket and left the shelter under the broken tree. Her spirits were low and the rain did not help. She was so sore and tired she didn't know if she could walk a mile, but she pushed herself to keep moving quickly through the woods. Miles passed. Each mile ahead was plagued with the question: Could she last another mile? Then that mile would pass and the question still remained. Suddenly it seemed like a light shone through the thick forest. She moved toward the light and soon came out of the trees. In front of her was a river. She dropped her pack. Her tired legs gave out and she fell to the ground and sat there. The rain had slowed, coming down as a fine mist. She could not swim this river but she could not stop. Standing, wobbling, walking once again, she moved down the river and was glad to find a log jam that helped the beavers make a bog across the flat land. Great sheets of water were surrounded by the beaver dams and the dams were surrounded by water. Beneath the sheets of shallow water deep saturated soil gave way and she sank in mud up to her knees. At times she was afraid she would not have the strength to pull herself free. To reach the logs she had to pull herself along on hanging branches and propel herself to the next high ground with a stick peeled smooth by beaver. She learned to stay beside the trees where the roots would prevent her from sinking. Across the bogs and dams she moved until she came to the great log jam. Then she cried and shook as she dragged John's rifle past spillways that moved with tremendous power through the logs. She knew that falling would be certain death: She would be pressed against the logs by the weight of the water. It would only take a few seconds for her to drown. When she reached the beaver bogs on the other side of the little river she sobbed with shoulders shaking. It had taken all day long to walk a mile.

But she was alive.

She rested for an hour until her body no longer quivered with fatigue. Then she used John's rifle to push her tired body upright, and she walked some more. She could not stop. She must walk.

As the days grew into weeks she walked. The woods changed. Where fires had burned the forest was clean and easy to walk through, ticks and mosquitoes were fewer, young growth was more fruitful. On she walked across the pleasant parts of the forest where tree trunks were charred by wild fires until she came to great dark regions of forest. Then she climbed over and through fallen trees in a land so rich that trees became great giants. The trees had laced their branches together and filled the sky with leaves. Sunlight arrived in only in specks and spots to lie gleaming on the forest floor by day. By night the forest was gloomy black even when the moon was bright. The darkness of summer stayed over this forest land until winter would blow the leaves away; a darkness that allowed nothing to grow below it. Tens of thousands of acres of virgin forest land supported no brush or thickets. But there were always trees. A thousand years of fallen trees littered the shade beneath a high green ceiling supported by columns of wood. Mounds of rot that had once been trees were crowned with dried and decaying trees a half a century old. Newly fallen trees, pushed down by twisting winds after five hundred years of standing tall lay atop the old. Trees fell with roots projecting twenty feet into the air: The massive towering roots would grip several tons of mud and dirt until the rain of a hundred years washed it away. Great pits were formed where trees had torn the soil from the ground as they fell to crush and break the rotting trees below. Over this tangle of pitted fragrant dark decay she climbed day after day.

When she walked the trails of the buffalo and deer that meandered around those ancient obstacles, she was afraid. Those same paths were trod by warriors. The paths were where Indian hunters waited to kill their prey. When she saw animal tracks pressed flat by human footprints she became afraid, but when she became frightened of the trails she must fight the trees again. Or stop. But she would not stop. Her fingernails were ripped apart from climbing past the towering roots and fallen trees. Her knees were scuffed down to blood and flesh. Her legs became bruised until the pains became sharp, vibrating, and constant. If her pain would make sounds loud enough to her, those sounds would be high pitched and pulsing. When she hurt too much to fight the trees, she would resign herself to walking in the trails again. Then she would walk the easy paths . . .afraid.

At night the wolves would howl. At first she was afraid to sleep. She was covered with scratches and her own blood smeared her clothing. She thought the wolves would smell her and find her. As the days passed by she fell asleep from weariness and wakened only when the wolves were very close. In the great dark unburned woods the wolves would sometimes follow her for miles. She would look back to see half a dozen wolves patiently panting along the path behind her. They did the same thing to bands of buffalo she saw: Enemies living in the same house together. She thought it must be the same way the devil had followed her until she became weak and murdered Yellow Hand. The wolves would follow all their prey until a weakness made them attack. They would attack her if they thought they could. But they always tired of following and always left when they saw or smelled some weaker creature than herself. She had grown to fear them less and less.

She saw bears. Black bears and rusty colored bears that ran away; bears that stood to look at her curiously; dangerous bears with little ones - that woofed out their warning; stay away! She knew those bears were dangerous because they had little ones, and she could not forget how she had killed a man because harm came to her son. The bears who led their soft black babies away from her made her cry: It seemed the mother bears already knew how dangerous she could be.

She saw a panther once, but she was sure they watched her all the time.

She would never know why they did not attack. She was obviously weaker than any animal around and smelled of blood and tiredness.

Moving a little south, but mostly east she walked. She shot very seldom, afraid an Indian hunter would hear the shot. But she ate. Meat was cooked and packed along until it began to stink. Her skin became chapped and red, swollen from a thousand insect bites. She would smear gobs of mud across her bare skin to discourage the mosquitoes. Her hair became matted and filthy. So she burned it short so she could wash it in the streams. She knew she must look like a animal, but it didn't matter. Short hair didn't slow her down. With John's gun she could get food, and with food she had strength. With enough strength she could walk.

She walked east until she came to a river that could only be the Ohio River. It was impossible to swim, but she didn't want to go farther south anyway. So she followed the river, always moving east. Sometimes she had to walk upstream when creeks and little rivers spilling into the Ohio blocked her path. Far above the place where the water emptied into the Ohio she'd find a way to cross and then move east once again.

The weeks passed and she became familiar with the silent forest where the loudest sounds were her own footfalls or her breath. She became familiar with the smells; buds and flowers; living animals and dead ones too; the smell of water; the rank odor of skunks; the strong smell of bears. She smelled smoke at times and moved carefully until she could know what caused the smoke, then she would walk for miles to go around. She never knew who made those fires but she knew that no one who made a fire would be her friend, so she walked around the smell of smoke.

She stopped making fires at night because she had become aware of how smoke could mark her whereabouts. A quick fire to cook her meat was all she allowed herself, then she would cover the ashes deep in dirt and move as many miles away as she could before the darkness fell. Without a fire the animals came much closer to her sleeping places, but none had dared to get too close. She supposed the smell of burnt black powder in John's gun was keeping them afraid.

The leaves were deep summer green when the river turned north. She could not cross the river, so she turned north as well. The land became steep and hilly, no longer as flat as it was before. Little streams fell down stony beds making noise that covered up the silence. The noise of the water made it hard to hear the forest around her. She had grown to like the silence and walked far from the noisy streams when she could. She had also noticed how the sounds made by water carried other sounds to her. The noisy water carried the sounds of animals, and even human voices, very clearly. She didn't want the sounds she made to be carried to the ears of hunters or fighters. She would rest only beside still waters so she could hear if someone was coming.

Still waters..."He maketh me to lie down in green pastures...he leadeth me beside still waters..."

Rachel wondered if God was leading her beside still water. She had walked hundreds of miles through a land of wolves and deadly men, and yet she was still alive to rest beside still waters. Would God really help someone like her? Would he help a murderer? She did not know for sure, but she did know one thing; she was walking across an unmapped continent and she was still alive. And increasingly she was becoming less afraid.

The river came from the north, so she moved north while the river remained an obstacle to her progress to the east. She walked north for days until she began to see moccasin tracks. Then she slowed and watched, sometimes for half an hour before she moved across an open wood, sometimes for two hours before she crossed a stream. More foot prints were present as she moved north. Then even more. She knew she must cross the river before she could be seen and taken from her course by painted men.

· · ·

Kitcheogeemaw found Yellowhand.

He had tried to prepare himself for the confrontation he knew must come. For days he tried to think of ways to end the meanness and arrogance of Yellowhand without a fight...or death. He did not want to kill his fellow tribesman, but he must stop Yellowhand from harming Catches-The-Wind. He knew Yellowhand too well to believe there was a way all this vengeance could end without bloodshed.

He was wrong.

Ten days from the village he found Yellowhand: the man was returning to the village. The scabs had fallen from the wounds Rachel had inflicted and Yellowhand's paint was smeared and rubbed away. He was moving quickly, too quickly, as he returned on the path he had taken. He was almost up to Kitcheogeemaw before he was aware of him. The man was so shocked to see Kitcheogeemaw that his body tensed like a bowstring pulled almost to the point of breaking. But the tension lasted only seconds before he recognized Kitcheogeemaw.

Over all these miles Kitcheogeemaw had expected bloodshed when they met. He did not expect a smile. Yellowhand was so relieved to no longer be alone that he could not hide his pleasure. He had followed the girl for all these days and had grown tired. He was tired of the toil; tired of the silence; tired of being careful in this land where other men could kill him and where no one would know he died. He was tired of crawling over giant trees so he would not lose Rachel's tracks when she left the easy paths. He didn't think about how the girl could stand such things because he thought only of himself. But he was glad to see a fellow tribesman, even if it was Kitcheogeemaw.

They greeted one another in that vast land where tribes were all that mattered. Then they sat together and talked. Kitcheogeemaw told Yellowhand that he was trying to find Catches-the-Wind. Yellowhand told about the war parties he had dodged and snakes that struck at him but missed. He told about the wolves that almost licked his feet at night. He told about how he wanted to bring Rachel back where she belonged. He lied, but that is what he said.

Kitcheogeemaw knew the things Yellowhand told were lies, but they did not harm him because he knew the truth. He knew Yellowhand was afraid. He'd seen him rushing too quickly, home.

Later Yellowhand slept while Kitcheogeemaw kept watch. As he watched in the twilight he thought about this mean man beside him. Could it be that this meanness was caused by a fearful heart? He began to remember things he hadn't really noticed until now. He thought how Yellowhand was never alone as long as he was sober. How he was brave only when people were watching. How he was mean when no one admired him. It didn't matter now. Rachel was safe from his meanness.

When the sun began to glow Kitcheogeemaw woke Yellowhand. He whispered about how he wanted Yellowhand to return to the village; how he must go on because the girl was his sister and how he must bring her home or know if she'd been killed by one of the war parties that Yellowhand had bragged of avoiding. But Kitcheogeemaw said that Yellowhand must return to the village, no matter how much he wanted to continue on this journey. He should go to tell Jacob that he would catch the girl. He said to tell Jacob that though Yellowhand might be willing, one man could pass more safely and it is what Kitcheogeemaw asked him to do.

Yellowhand knew he could not inflict his vengeance on the girl while Kitcheogeemaw was nearby. He knew he was tired of chasing the girl through this dangerous land. He hadn't really seen an enemy, but there could be many up ahead, and he and Kitcheogeemaw were only two people; and Kitcheogeemaw could run faster...he would get away while Yellowhand would be caught. Yellowhand built a dozen imaginary and evil endings for himself and agreed that he should go back with the message and let Kitcheogeemaw go on alone.

So they parted without bloodshed. Relieved, Kitcheogeemaw watched the fearful man retreat back to the village. Then he turned to follow Rachel. He would find his sister...

CHAPTER TWENTY NINE

Rachel's journey had ended.

Across the great river was the peeled tree. She could not see the painted figures from this distance, but she knew there was a red X on it that represented herself. It was the tree where John had screamed out all his love for her. It was his tree and hers. The painted warriors had made it for a memorial to themselves, and to death and suffering, but it had become a memorial to love: Her love and John's.

It was only across the river, but it might as well have been a thousand miles away. The river might as well have been made of molten iron: It was impossible to cross. She could not swim and there was no one to help her. She sat and cried back in the underbrush that always grows where rivers let in light. Her journey was done.

She had cried many times in the last months but now she cried so hard her whole body shook. Tears washed down her face but could not wash the misery away. She was alone. When she was here, back when the tree was freshly peeled, she was surrounded by men who would kill her. She was afraid and heartbroken, but her enemies were with her and she was not alone. The last time she was here she could look beside that bark less tree and see John and Nemesis and Tom. They couldn't reach her and she could not go to them, but she was not alone. Even when she could no longer see the tree, or John, she was not alone because when the men shoved her away from him into the curtain of trees she still had a baby growing inside her. Now the Indians were gone, John was gone, and the baby was gone. She was alone . . .

She sat surrounded by the tracks of warriors with her back to a continent that didn't care. Jacob and Little Fawn were now so far away that it seemed they must live only in someone else's life. She could not go back. She could not go on.

. . .

Kicheogeemaw could not follow quickly. He must be careful. Yellowhand had been so afraid of the danger in this country he would not go on, but Kitcheogeemaw knew he must follow Rachel. Fear could not reign in him, fear would not be allowed to rule him, but still he must be careful.

Catches-The-Wind had made it difficult to follow. If she stayed to the paths like any other woman he could have caught her easily, but she left the paths for days at a time, and he had to follow. The dark land she crossed was very difficult, but if he did not follow he could lose her tracks and would not be able to find them again.

So he followed.

. . .

Rachel ate the roasted back-strap of deer with cooked roots of thistles. A certain peacefulness made the meal special. It seemed like forever since she had eaten so well or rested so free of fear...or guilt.

It took two days before she could make herself leave the peeled tree. But she became hungry. Crying did not float her across the river and her life did not end because she could not go; so she became hungry. But she could not hunt in this place. She still had the rifle. She enjoyed the polished surface of the maple gun stock because she knew that John had touched and rubbed it for hours to make it gleaming and smooth. She cherished the leaves and curls his fingers had carved along the wrist and at the place where the ramrod slid into the wood. She liked to feel the cool metal that he had shaped and filed to make the lock move with such precision...but the gun was a danger to her here where so many warriors crossed the river: If they heard her shoot they would find her. She could not hunt here. Packing her things, she moved down the river. Her heart broke all over again when she looked back at the pale tree growing more distant with each step. She would come back, but first she must eat.

She had almost decided to sit across from the pale lonely tree until some painted man came along to kill her. Then she thought how far she'd come and yet remained alive; even remained strong. She could not imagine such a thing was possible if God had not helped. She was convinced that for some reason God had helped, and though she did not deserve it, maybe he would help her more. But she would never know if she sat here until someone killed her. She must try to stay live. But not here. Hunger would make her wait downriver, away from this warrior path, where she could hunt. She would stay alive and see if God would help.

Two days later she sat across the river from where a sheer steep cliff ranged north and south for miles. No one could cross the river here so the paths were nearly empty of moccasin tracks. Only the tracks of bears and deer and wolves were seen. She hunted. She no longer had to walk each day so she took time to find a secluded place where she would not need to hide the parts of the deer she could not eat. Such remains would betray her presence if someone saw them before the wolves and buzzards could devour them. She had time to take care of her gear. John's rifle was carefully kept clean and dry and loaded. She tended the gun as lovingly as she would care for John if she could. And the rifle fed her so well that she grew strong again; just as John would feed her if he could. More days passed.

She returned to the pale painted tree, hoping to see some white hunter on the river. But she never did. War must be still be raging to keep the hunters from the river so completely. Moccasin tracks told her this was true. The war path was becoming smooth and worn at the crossing by the tree. After a ways, she moved back down the river to hunt, and eat, and sleep.

She washed herself. Her hair required several days of washing before it glistened in the puddles she used for mirrors. Her skin healed of scratches. It took only a few days of care and rest to undo the damage her body had suffered. If only her soul could be healed as easily. She still loathed herself for the accusation of murder that followed her like the wolves. It had followed her from the village and accused her here as well. She washed and washed, but only her skin and hair would come clean.

She had time to find other food than meat. She found a butternut tree but it was still to early in the year to eat. She found a squirrel's stash of hickory nuts that hadn't spoiled from the rain. She found thistles and dug the roots and peeled the stems. Berries would soon be ripe so she marked where they were growing when she found them. She rested, hunted, ate, . . .and thrived. She grew strong instead of weak. She washed her blanket because she had time, and washed her clothes as well. But she still longed to wash her soul.

Then one day she woke up and a verse came to her lips. She spoke aloud for the first time in a long time and recited a verse she learned as a child. "Blessed is he whose transgression is forgiven, whose sin is covered. Blessed is the man unto whom the Lord imputeth not iniquity, and in whose spirit there is no guile..." That day she repeated the memory verse over and over. And she understood it deeply for the first time in her life. Blessed indeed. Men may sacrifice and idolize; they may clean themselves and their houses until no dirt remains; they may have the good opinion of other men; but guilt is not a thing that can be touched or washed of lifted by hands. It cannot be cleaned by anything man can do. But forgiveness can cleanse. When she remembered the verse that quoted God, she began to understand that God was not a tyrant who used holiness as a club. God said, "I will be merciful to their unrighteousness and remember their sins and their iniquities no more." He did not say that as long as she remembered her iniquities he would too. God's love and forgiveness did not depend on her. It depended only on God. She began to understand that God is truly love, and love could cover anything he wanted. So she loved God more than ever.

That was the day she used the clasp knife to carve a cross into the maple stock.

She boiled her thistles and roasted fresh deer meat that day, then she covered the fire with many inches of dirt and moved several miles to eat. She sat with John's gun across her lap and ate the food it provided. This was the same gun she used to kill a man awakening from a drunken stupor. But it was just wood and iron. This same gun could only do good or bad depending on the hand that held it. She was the one who killed. But God still loved her. As she took a bite of thistle she knew she could be cleaned too. She was glad she could remember that many accounts told how Jesus was asked to heal - and how he healed, with forgiveness.

And so she thrived.

. . .

Kitcheogeemaw was fighting through the maze of trees that held Rachel's tracks when he suddenly knew where to find her. He no longer had to follow every track. He had been aware for some time that the trail was mostly due east, deviating only when a river got in the way. The rivers always made her go around another way, or follow upstream until they narrowed enough to cross. But there was a river she would not be able to cross. She would go up that river as far as she wanted to and there was no crossing for a woman who could not swim. He knew she would go up the river until she saw that tree.

Then she would stop. The river would make her stop but the tree would hold her there. He knew he would find her across from the peeled tree where he had painted her picture in red.

He fought his way out of the tangled woods and found a path. He must still go slow enough to be careful, but he could go much faster...now that he knew where she would be.

CHAPTER THIRTY

Phares Homestead

John held Lewis's hand still and steady while gently tapping the small carving tool. He was glad to see the little tongue stuck out as the boy concentrated and struggled to follow the line he had marked on the maple gun stock. Lewis was delighted when they brushed away the shavings and saw that the groove made by the tool was smooth and graceful.

"Can I do another one?"

John found a scrap of wood and drew some flowers, curls and leaves. He clamped it down and handed Lewis the gouge. "Try it by yourself." Lewis took the tools and leaned into the work, sticking his tongue out the corner of his mouth again as he began to tap. John watched over his shoulder, reaching out to steady the small hands, or pull the tools to a more appropriate angle. "Not bad, Lewis." He stepped back. "Now you are on your own. But you can do it."

John left the boy and stepped to the door of the freshly finished gun shop and looked out at the evening light.

John never really recovered from Yellowhand's news of Rachel's death. Recovery would mean going back to some semblance of the life that had gone on before. His life would never be the same. The only thing that remained the same was the carving and shaping of wood and the forging of iron. The Indian trade was gone with the war. So John made guns. The intense work kept him from thinking about how Rachel must have suffered. It wasn't easy to live anymore.

Lewis helped him live. Tom must have known that he would. He let the boy practically live with John. They would hunt and plant and make guns together. Lewis loved it. Lewis would almost forget to put up his guard sometimes and before he caught himself would lean his head against John's arm. Lewis was beginning to love again. He never really stopped loving the people around him, but he had kept himself from betraying his true feelings with touch or expression. But that was changing.

Lewis exclaimed, "What do you think of this John?"

John peered at the grooves that lined the maple wood and said, "You do carve a beautiful flower. Let me draw you some more."

"Can I make flowers better than any other boy?"

"I can honestly say that I have never seen a boy carve flowers as good as yours. Now, you keep on like this and you'll be making better flowers than any gun maker I know."

John clamped the newly marked wood onto the workbench and handed the tools to Lewis again. This time as he walked to the door he smiled: the sun was close to setting and instead of speaking of death or killing all day long, Lewis had spoken only of flowers.

•   •   •

Kitcheogeemaw rested in the brush along the river directly across from the peeled tree. He was puzzled. He was sure that she would be here. He'd arrived two days ago but didn't find her. Not even tracks. He went upstream to see if she had passed. He went downstream but saw nothing. No campfires, no carcass of deer or bear, no place where roots were being dug. Nothing that would indicate she had passed this way. The only thing here were the tracks of hundreds of warriors that had been raiding over across the river.

Kitcheogeemaw was not foolish enough to think he was safe here: Many tribes were making war and not all of them loved the Wyandots. Some of them would kill him as quickly as they would a white man. So he hid. He may not know what to do with Rachel, but he knew enough to hide. He would wait for another day or two. Maybe it was just as well: He needed time to think. If he found her he would want to take her home, but he did not know if that was right anymore. Catches-The-Wind was not a slave. She was his sister - free to do anything she wanted to do. Still, Little Fawn wanted a daughter, and he knew Jacob had never been as fond of another living creature. And he had not come all this way for nothing.

He had been so sure she would be here. What if she had found a way to cross the river? Her tracks could be just beneath that tree.

He watched a fisher bird dive toward the river and skim across the top then fly back to a dead branch devoid of leaves. It sat there for a moment then made another dive, twisting in the air as it picked something from the water.

Kitcheogeemaw looked up the river and then down. He watched the paths while the fisher bird dived a dozen times. Then he picked up his trade gun and walked a long way up the river to find a tree that would make a small canoe. He decided he was going to cross the river to see if Rachel had passed the disfigured tree.

. . .

Rachel had become restless. She ate well. She rested often. She was no longer tired. But it was still too dangerous to move through the woods too much, so she sat still most of the day. She noticed how motion betrayed the deer. A deer could stand fifty yards away and remain invisible until it twitched an ear or tail. Grouse could hide and not be seen until they became frightened and moved from their hiding place. Rachel saw how movement cried out for attention so she learned be still.

She was using up black powder too quickly. The powder horn that contained and protected the precious supply from moisture had been shaved thin enough see that only 12 or 14 loads remained. When the powder was gone the gun would be useless. She thought she should kill only deer; she would get more meat per shot than if she killed small game or turkeys.

She spent much time by the river now. She was waiting for some white man to pass by in a boat. She even began to think she could build a raft and somehow propel it across this powerful divide. How could she get across without being seen? The raft would surely travel many miles downstream before she could get across. And what if some Indian sat against the bank - like she did - waiting for whoever might pass by? Perhaps she might try to make a bark canoe like the one made from the peeled tree. She had tried to peel bark from different trees but nothing seemed to work.

She must do something soon. She getting low on powder.

. . .

Kitcheogeemaw crossed the river the following day. He had found an elm tree far north of the warrior path, peeled its bark and made a make shift canoe. It was smaller than the one they made with the bark from painted tee, but it carried him across the river safely.

At the tree there were no tracks small enough to belong to Catches-The-Wind.

Kitcheogeemaw hadn't thought of any possibility other than finding Catches-The-Wind. He did not think it was possible for a woman to elude him. He still didn't think it was possible. He was so convinced that he began to accept another possibility: she had been killed somewhere in the dark woods and he had passed her by. The only reason that would explain why she wasn't attracted to the peeled tree was death. He thought only death would stop her from coming here.

The thought made his mind as dark as the clouds that moved in slowly from the west. A sharp wind reminded him that if he was going to return across the river he must move quickly. There was nothing here to hold him. No tracks. No girl.

He fought the wind to cross the river. Waves rippled harshly and splashed him. Then the wind would change and push him from behind. Lightning began to flash below the clouds. As he came to shore lightning cracked behind him. It was so close it left the taste of copper in his mouth. Rain began to fall in torrents and he grabbed his gun and fled. He turned around only once to see the tree once more. As lightning flashed he saw the tree stark white against its darker brothers - as flames from the lightning strike lingered in its crown. Then Kitcheogeemaw turned and ran west on the warrior path while the rain washed away his tracks.

He must go home to tell his tribe...

Catches-The-Wind is no more...

· · ·

Rachel hid as the wind made noise in the branches that almost rivaled the loudness of the thunder. Lightning flashed against wet leaves and glistened like uncountable fireplace sparks. Trees lifted up and then bent down as though some giant invisible foot were stepping on them. The wind pressed down hard upon the river, but Rachel was not hiding from the wind. There was no place to hide anyway. She was hiding from the form she saw running into the forest.

She knew it was an Indian. She'd seen his scalp-lock as he bent his head against the wind and rain. Then the world turned blinding white as lightning ripped apart her tree. Branches fell, and fire cast an orange glow on surrounding trees. But rain came down much stronger then, and the fire could not withstand it. The flames died out and when she looked for the warrior he was gone.

She stayed still in the trees and brush and watched the land across the river. She had plugged the barrel of the rifle with a stick and the touch-hole with a blue Jay feather. Even in this rainstorm the powder charge was safe. But the rain began to make her cold and lightning flashed and flashed so fast it seemed it was the darkness that was flashing - to interrupt the light. So swiftly did the lightning flash that the world was bright and she could see clearly. No other warrior could be found on the other bank. As thunder cracked and rumbled she looked up and down the river to see if any other warrior moved there. There was nothing. But there was a shadow on the water.

The canoe.

The Indian had abandoned it and it was becoming full of water and moving from the shore. The wind blew waves that pushed it one way and then another as it moved downstream. Before the lightning flashed again the place where Rachel hid was empty: she was gone -she was running down the river through the woods as fast as she could go. She could not let the canoe be taken by the river.

A tree crashed to the ground behind her. A branch fell just ahead. Still she ran and leaped with slender legs to catch the boat before it blew away. Downstream she flew behind a screen of brush until she could get closer to the river. Her hair was streaming water and she held the rifle like shield to deflect branches that tried to hold her back. Then at a place where the land dipped down to meet the river she slid down to the water's edge. The storm-blackened river seemed to seethe and boil under the lash of the horrific rain. She slid and staggered to a stop, ankle deep in water that already seemed to want to pull her under. Her chest heaved as she breathed and felt her heart was pounding hard. Lightning flashed and she saw the boat - just out of reach- in the black water.

The roiling water concealed the depth of her next steps. The blackness of the heavy water seemed to hiss as it went by and pulled the boat downstream. One more step and she could die.

Before she thought, she threw the gun against the bank far out of the waters reach and before she could take another breath she had thrown herself into the depths she did not know...

her fingers caught the edges of the bark...

One finger slipped, then another. Then she dug in with bending, cracking, tearing fingernails and pulled herself to embrace the half sunken canoe...as it drifted down the river.

She tried to climb in the canoe and almost pulled it under, so she hung on with one hand and reached toward the bank with the other. She did not know how far she drifted in the lightning and thunder that seemed to add greater violence to the cold water all around her. Thunder crushed down on her ears like a firing line of overcharged rifles. Lightning still lit up the sky and painted the dark water grey as iron for split seconds that seemed to never end. She hoped to catch a tree top that had been toppled in the water. She hoped to catch a hank of grass flattened by the wind. All she caught was water.

Instead of waiting for the branches or the grass she began to use her hand as though it were a paddle. Then the wind blew hard toward the shore, and she felt her feet touch the muddy bottom of the river. With every muscle straining he pulled and pushed until she lay exhausted on the water's edge while the storm still pounded all around her.

Now she knew. And she would always know ... she could get across the river.

An hour later the rumbles of thunder were becoming softer in the distance as Rachel stood beneath the painted tree. She had her rifle in her hands as she watched the canoe float down the river. It was just a speck of bark that she no longer valued. It had served its purpose. Now she could go to John.

She moved quickly to the tree. She did not need to go to it. But she wanted to. The lightning had split it to the roots, but it still stood. Some of its branches were dead because the tree had been robbed of its bark. Some of the branches were set on fire by the lightning and were charred and black. Some of its branches held up wilted leaves that died when lightning struck, but some branches were still strong and some leaves were still vibrant.

The painting had been washed by snow and rain since she had been here. It seemed so long ago. Every mark was faded ... except one. She reached up to touch the red lines that formed her X, and slick greasy vermilion stained her finger: The picture of herself had been freshly repainted. Instantly she searched the ground for tracks, but there was only mud. There was no chance of finding the foot prints belonging to whoever refreshed the paint. With wonder she looked up again. For several minutes she watched the far bank but no one could be seen. She searched the ground again and saw a stone that had escaped her notice. Another stone lay atop, but beneath that top stone, held tight above the mud and protected from the rain, lay a pouch of leather.

She rolled the top stone away and took the leather in her hand. Her skin began to draw tight like goose flesh and she looked around again. She had been so long hidden in the forest that she began to feel uneasy in the open light beneath the tree. So she looked once more to the west and moved quickly to the covering forest. She could still see the tree when she stopped again. The footprints she left behind were already half dissolved by the falling rain. No one would ever know she stopped. No one would ever know she stood there.

The sky was growing steadily brighter while the rain still fell, though much more quietly than before. It fell onto the leaves above her and rolled from leaf to leaf until much larger drops were formed before they fell to earth. Rachel untied the strings that bound the leather pouch, unrolled the case and shook it until a little Bible fell into her hand.

A big drop of water fell from an oak leaf up above and splashed on the leather cover, so she bent low to catch the rain against her body...to protect the little book. She tried to wipe her hand free of wetness before she opened it. There on the first blank page she saw two names, Sutton, and Jacob Otter...Water fell again and wet the page. But it was not water from the sky. The water came from her eyes as she recognized a gift from her beloved Jacob. Before more tears could wet the rest of the page she closed the book and wrapped it tight again. She stowed it in her shooting pouch, and stood up straight again to breathe, and looked back at the tree.

When she had been taken past this tree against her will she knew that all she cherished would be fenced away by this great river. But she was wrong. She hadn't known that she would find things to cherish on the other side. Now she knew that this great barrier could never fence out love. Now she knew.

Though great dark forests covered this unmapped land and rivers flowed like great divides, though men and murder served the darkest hearts, nothing could defeat love.

Her hand moved unconsciously to touch the swell where the Bible rested in the shooting pouch and knew she had love...love to find and know...on both sides of every river. Taking John's gun in her hand she turned into the woods. She walked carefully, but confidently into the mountains, moving east. She thought about how surprised John would be to see her...to know the rifle given as a gift to a deceitful man...had brought her home again.

EPILOGUE

As a handyman cleaned up all the broken glass he found the baseball, and in the rafters just above it, he found the old flintlock rifle with carved curls and leaves on its maple stock. He took time to pull it from the rafters and brush away the dust and grime. A smooth polished surface still gleamed between deep scratches. In the slanted light he could see some barely readable letters engraved atop the rusty barrel — "John Phares" —. Someone had carved a crude cross along the stock. It marred the beauty of the carving, but it had been there for a long, long time. A moth-eaten blue Jay feather was still jammed in the old flint locks touch hole. The flint was missing.

When he was finished the job he took the gun downstairs and asked the woman if she knew anything about it. She said she had never see that gun in her whole life. She said she didn't like guns at all. The handyman asked if she would sell it.

"Tell you what," she said, "If you take that gun for fixing the window I'll call it square...It probably ain't worth a thing at all and I don't want guns around here anyway.

In the attic the light shone brightly through new glass. The dust of a hundred years had been cleaned away and though the workman's truck was almost to the mailbox, flecks of dust still lingered in the air. One small fleck, so tiny it would sit on the sharp end of a pin, was lifted up on sun warmed air. It floated deeper into the attic and then began to fall. It came to rest against a leather pouch that held a Bible. One day, if the old house still stood, someone would brush that fleck of dust away and read the page still stained with a teardrop.

—To Jacob Otter from B. Sutton—

Then they would read the tear stained words below.

—Catches-The-Wind—

My people took you captive to bring love back to us. Now you have captured all our hearts. We have loved you and we always will...

—Jacob—

There were no tear stains on the faded ink below Jacob's name. There were just the names of John and Rachel's six daughters, and the names of a dozen grand children had been written down there until there was no more space to write.

THE END

Purchase other Black Rose Writing titles at www.blackrosewriting.com/books

and use promo code PRINT to receive a 20% discount.

BLACK❦ROSE
writing™

CPSIA information can be obtained at www.ICGtesting.com
Printed in the USA
BVOW05s1329300416

446074BV00001B/7/P

9 781612 966854